"You had to spend the night with Peter's group?" Chrissy asked. "Wasn't that a fate worse than death?"

"Not quite," Caroline _____

"Why co____ _____ ____ __?" Chrissy blur____ ____ ____ _____ ____ ou don't even li__ ___

Caroline ke__ ____ _____ ____ back onto her bed a__ ____ _____bbing at her rash again. "Boy, th__ poison oak is miserable," she said. "I didn't even feel this bad with the chicken pox."

I can't tell her now, Caroline thought. *She's feeling bad enough as it is. I'll let her find out gradually, when she's up and about again.*

"I'm going to eat breakfast," she said. "And then I'm going to take a long nap. See you later."

"Sure, Cara. See you later," Chrissy said, climbing back into bed. She looked so small and helpless lying there that Caroline was seized by feelings of guilt.

Stop being so dumb, she told herself. *You like Peter. Peter likes you. It's as simple as that. Chrissy really doesn't come into this at all!*

Other books in the **SUGAR & SPICE** series:

\# 1 Two Girls, One Boy
\# 2 Trading Places
\# 3 The Last Dance
\# 4 Dear Cousin
\# 5 Nothing in Common
\# 6 Flip Side

COMING SOON:

\# 8 Surf's Up!
\# 9 Double Take
\#10 Make Me A Star

Janet Quin-Harkin's

Sugar & Spice

Tug of War

IVY BOOKS • NEW YORK

Ivy Books
Published by Ballantine Books
Copyright © 1987 by Butterfield Press, Inc. & Janet Quin-Harkin

Produced by Butterfield Press, Inc.
133 Fifth Avenue
New York, New York 10003

Library of Congress Catalog Card Number: 87-90921

ISBN 0-8041-0058-6

Manufactured in the United States of America

First Edition: November 1987

TUG OF WAR

Janet Quin-Harkin

Chapter 1

"I still can't believe we're seniors!" Chrissy Madden exclaimed, looking up from the middle of her bed, where she was surrounded by a mountain of sweaters, hundreds of mismatched socks, a prom dress, and several pairs of sneakers, covered with a snowstorm of loose pieces of notebook paper.

Caroline Kirby, her cousin and roommate for the past year, looked up from her desk by the window, where she was busy writing a neat list. "We're not seniors for three more months," she said. Her eyes opened wide in horror as she surveyed the disaster area opposite her. "*Mon dieu*, Chrissy, what are you doing?"

"Deciding what to take home to Iowa and what to take with me on my backpacking trip," Chrissy

1

said calmly. "And we are too seniors. You move up a class the day school ends. So we are now two mature high school seniors."

Caroline grinned. "I take it that organization doesn't come with maturity?" she asked.

"Didn't you know that clutter and disorganization were signs of super creativity—the work of a genius?" Chrissy said, leaning back against the mountain of mess.

"Some genius," Caroline giggled, shaking her head as she gazed at the fluttering papers. "The fact that most of your papers have hearts on them with C loves J in the middle definitely indicates a genius at work!"

"None of my papers have hearts on them!" Chrissy said hotly, snatching at the papers and hurriedly hiding a couple. "Well, most of them don't! These are all chemistry notes. Think of it, Cara—I won't need them ever again. I could throw them all out of the window and watch them float down the hill and into the Bay."

"I don't think so somehow," Caroline said, unsure whether Chrissy was joking or not. "The San Francisco police are not very understanding about littering, except on New Year's Day. You don't want to spend your hard-earned savings on a giant fine instead of a trip to the mountains, do you?"

"Are you kidding? I've been looking forward to this trip for weeks." Chrissy began to gather the papers into a pile and stuff them into a grocery bag. "I'm glad that I saw the notice on the school bulletin board. I just wish a couple more people from Maxwell had signed up. Oh well—at least I'll get to meet people from other schools."

Caroline looked at her cousin with understanding. "I'm sure you'll fit right in," she said. "Last year everyone had a ball. I really wish I could come with you, but the job was too good to turn down. High school students don't usually get counselor's jobs at summer camps. They usually only take college students. It was lucky that Tracy's dad knew the owner and put in a good word for us." She gazed down at the mimeographed page in front of her, a long list of everything she would need for a whole summer away from home. The thought of two months up in the mountains in charge of little kids was scary, but exciting at the same time. "It's going to be such fun," she said out loud, as much to reassure herself as to inform Chrissy.

Chrissy nodded. "It will be great," she said. "You'll be with Tracy, and you'll be getting paid for swimming and getting a great tan—"

"And looking after a lot of little kids," Caroline reminded her. "There is some work involved too, Chrissy."

"I know, but it will still be fun," Chrissy said. "I almost wish that I had decided to stay on all summer and come with you, but I really should be getting back home and picking up my old life. If I went straight to my old school from California, it would be too much of a culture shock. Besides, my mom misses me and wants to spend some time with me before school starts."

Caroline smiled at her cousin. "Just think, Chrissy—you'll be going home to the job of head cheerleader. And you'll be a celebrity—the girl who's been to California. Everyone will gaze at you in admiration!"

Chrissy shrugged her shoulders. "I guess so," she said hesitantly. She rose from the bed—and an avalanche of socks and papers fell to the floor. "It's dumb, you know," she said, walking across the room to gaze out the window. "I've been dreaming of this moment all year. I could imagine exactly how it would be to go home again and enjoy being a Danbury, Iowa, big shot. But now that the moment has almost arrived, I don't know if I want to go."

"You think you'll miss California too much?"

"I know I'll miss California," Chrissy said. "I'll miss being able to look out at a view like this and going to the latest movies and eating out and talking with my new friends. I know I'll miss all that. But it doesn't keep me from being scared about whether senior year back home will be as perfect as I've always dreamed it would be. Now that I've lived in San Francisco and been to Maxwell High, somehow being head cheerleader back home doesn't seem like such a big deal."

"I'm sure it will be, Chrissy," Caroline said. "I'm sure you'll really get a kick out of all the attention."

Chrissy turned and gave Caroline a big grin. "That's for sure," she said. "You know me—I was always a sucker for attention!" She walked over to Caroline's desk and peered over her shoulder. "Is that all you're taking?" she asked in horror. "For two whole months?"

Caroline surveyed the list critically. "It's a summer camp," she said. "What more would I need?"

"What if there are some really cute male counselors? Won't you want to impress them a little?"

"All the male counselors will probably be horrible, healthy jocks who do push-ups before breakfast," Caroline said.

"Boy, you are a pessimist," Chrissy said.

"Just a realist," Caroline said calmly, going back to her list. "And why must you always try to put romance into every situation? You are boy-crazy, Chrissy Madden. You'd even fall in love with your dentist if he smiled when he said, 'Open wide!' "

"I would not!" Chrissy answered. "I was just thinking that it's about time you found a new love in your life."

"I still have Roger," Caroline pointed out.

Chrissy frowned. "Roger is very nice," she said slowly. "He's great for teaching you about marine biology and the aquatic ecosystem, but you have to admit, you are not head over heels in love with him."

"So?" Caroline asked. "That sort of feeling doesn't come along too often. I'm comfortable with Roger. I enjoy his company. And I've already been head over heels once this year. Once was definitely enough. I still haven't picked up the pieces from my encounter with Luke."

"So you don't have to fall madly in love right away with a cute, tanned counselor," Chrissy insisted. "But that's no reason not to be prepared with a couple of great outfits, just in case!"

Caroline shook her head, laughing gently. "You're something else, Chrissy Madden," she said. "Finding a boy of your own isn't a big enough success for you; you have to spend your spare time matchmaking for me."

"I just want everyone to end up happy ever after," Chrissy said.

Caroline swiveled around in her chair. "And you think you and Jeff will be 'happy ever after'?"

Chrissy actually blushed, which was unusual for her. "Who knows," she said. "You know Jeff. He's the sort of person who lives for today. He is terrific to be with, but—oh, I just don't know, Cara. I will admit he is one of the main reasons I'm not rushing straight back to Iowa—once I go home, I'll never see him again."

Caroline eyed the pile of stuff on Chrissy's bed. "You won't see him if you go on this tour to the mountains," she said.

"While I'm gone, Jeff will be busy rehearsing with his new band. Isn't that terrific, Cara? Just think, this group might even make a video. If they become a big hit, I can say I actually dated a rock star!"

Caroline shook her head. "What I like about

you, Chrissy Madden, is that you never think small."

"Speaking of thinking small," Chrissy said, "do you think all this stuff will go in one backpack?"

"Including the prom dress and the chemistry notes?" Caroline asked with a giggle.

Chrissy shot Caroline her famous withering stare. "And why would I need a prom dress or chemistry notes on a backpacking trip around Lake Tahoe?" she asked.

"Who knows," Caroline said sweetly. "You might meet a cute ranger and be asked to the rangers' annual ball . . ."

"Be sensible, Caroline. You are supposed to be the sensible one, remember? I want to know if I'm taking too much to carry. I've never backpacked before."

"Is all this too much?"

"How long did you say you were going for?"

"About a week, I guess."

"But there must be ten sweaters here, and I can see three bikinis and every pair of jeans you own."

"So? I don't want to be too cold or too hot."

"Chrissy, be reasonable. You only need a change of jeans, a sweater, a jacket, and a few T-shirts. You'd stagger up the mountain with all that stuff on your back."

Chrissy sank back onto the bed. "Maybe you're right," she said. She gave a big sigh. "I'm beginning to think that this trip wasn't such a good idea," she said. "I really wanted to see Lake

Tahoe before I went home, but now I'm not so sure. If only you and Tracy weren't disappearing so quickly and Justine weren't going to Hawaii and Maria didn't have to work—"

"And Jeff weren't rehearsing," Caroline cut in.

"Instead, I'll probably meet Bigfoot and be eaten for breakfast or buried under an avalanche and nobody will ever know what happened to me."

Caroline got up and put her hand on her cousin's shoulder. "You always have to dramatize things, don't you?" she asked. "Lake Tahoe is a very safe place, Chrissy. It's full of tourists, there is no Bigfoot, there are no avalanches in June, and you can't get lost."

Chrissy smiled. "I guess you're right," she said. "Although I'm not so sure about Bigfoot." She lifted a wrinkled wad of fabric from the bed. "I'd better finish sorting these things or I won't be able to go to bed tonight," she said. "It's hard to imagine that this time next week we'll both be up in the mountains, you sitting around a campfire with a cute counselor, me being carried up a precipice by an inhuman monster."

Caroline laughed and threw a pillow at her cousin. "Think of whom you might meet. There will be guys from all over on this trip, and you'll love Tahoe. It's a great place."

Caroline watched as Chrissy started throwing items of clothing back into open drawers. *It's funny,* she thought, *but when Chrissy first came here, I thought there was nothing in the world that scared her. But now I know she's just as insecure and scared as I am.* She went back to her desk and drew a neat line across the bottom of her list. *Another funny thing,* Caroline thought, *is that I'm not particularly scared about going off to camp, although Chrissy seems to be having some doubts about her trip. Things have changed a lot over the past year.*

Chapter 2

Caroline flipped on the light switch as she entered the living room and gasped as she saw something move in the shadows next to the window.

"Caroline," her mother said. "Did I scare you?"

"My heart nearly stopped beating, that's all." Caroline managed a smile. "I just got here. I didn't know anyone else was home yet. What were you doing sitting in the dark?"

"I must have dozed off reading my book," her mother said, getting up from the couch.

Caroline walked to the window. "It's so pretty tonight, Mom. Look—the sun is winking back from all the windows across the Bay, and all the hills are glowing in the sunset."

Edith Kirby sat down on the window seat and

patted the spot beside her. Caroline smiled and sat down next to her. "You're awfully dreamy tonight, sweetie," her mother said. "Anything particular on your mind?" she asked.

"Lots of things," Caroline said, "little things really—like the fact that in two more days I'll be responsible for a lot of little kids. I hadn't really thought about the responsibility much before, but tonight I started thinking what I'd do if a kid got lost or tripped and broke an ankle . . ."

Her mother put a comforting hand on her shoulder. "Don't worry about it. Tracy will be right there, and her working in the day-care center has prepared her for those things. And don't forget, there will be senior counselors you can call on. It will be a wonderful experience and a big step toward growing up. Taking care of others shows that you are no longer a child yourself."

Caroline's mother sighed wistfully and reached out to pat her daughter's hand. "You're going to have a great time, honeybunch. That part of the Sierras is beautiful. And I promise we'll drive up and visit you sometime to take you out for real food!" her mother said with a laugh. She slid down from the seat. "Are you all packed? Your room looked like a cyclone hit it last time I peeked inside."

Caroline grinned. "I was packed days ago," she said. "So was Chrissy, but she keeps on changing her mind and unpacking. I think she's starting to realize that the school year really is over and soon she'll be back in Iowa. I think part of her would like to stay here with us."

Caroline's mother smiled. "I'm sure she'll be fine," she said. "She'll have a great time on this trip. Her father was a bit worried about the trip, but I reassured him that it was well supervised and safe. Besides, it you haven't seen the mountains, you haven't seen California."

"I hope she's a little careful, Mom," Caroline said, her forehead creasing into a worried frown. "Knowing Chrissy, she'll talk to everyone she meets, and she'll be getting offers from strangers to explore secret trails, complete with cozy, dark caves."

"Chrissy's not stupid, Caroline," Mrs. Kirby said firmly. "She has a lot of good old Iowa horse sense, you know. Where is she this evening, anyway?"

Caroline grinned. "She's with Jeff. Need I say more? They'll probably have a big farewell because she's going to be gone for a whole week.

"Strange how Chrissy and Jeff hit it off so well," Caroline's mother said. "I always thought he was the perfect boyfriend for you."

"He was, on paper," Caroline said. "A computer dating service would have matched us up instantly, but for some reason we never really were that attracted to each other."

"Never mind. Roger is a very nice boy," Mrs. Kirby said comfortingly.

Caroline nodded. "A nice boy," she said with a grin. "That's what all mothers want for their daughters, isn't it? You're right. Roger is a nice boy, but . . ." She trailed off, unable to say what exactly kept her from feeling more strongly about Roger.

"Too steady and reliable?" Mrs. Kirby asked with a raised eyebrow. "You are just like me, Caroline. You secretly crave excitement. That's why I married your father."

"Daddy?" Caroline shrieked, her face creasing into a big smile.

"Your father was a real radical when I met him at Berkeley," Mrs. Kirby said, a dreamy expression crossing her face. "He protested against everything! And he wore his hair very long."

Caroline giggled. "I just can't imagine my father as a radical with long hair," she said. "But I don't think I secretly crave excitement exactly. After all, for a teenager, Jeff is really pretty exciting—a star in the youth symphony, with his own rock group on the side. I know Chrissy thinks so. He's been the one boy she's really flipped over since she got here. She does nothing lately but talk about Jeff, Jeff, Jeff! I don't know how she's going to face leaving him."

"It won't be long now, will it?" Caroline's mother asked. "It will seem so strange with Chrissy gone." A faraway look came into her eyes.

"I know," Caroline said. "No doors slamming, nobody yelling and knocking things over and getting into impossible situations. It will be wonderfully peaceful again, *and* I'll have my parents' attention to myself once more."

Mrs. Kirby looked up sharply. "Sounds like you'll be glad when she's gone," she commented.

Caroline cocked her head thoughtfully to one side. She hadn't meant to sound so enthusiastic about it. "In a way I will be glad," she agreed. "It will be nice to have a room and family to myself again. But I have a feeling it will seem awfully quiet around here when Chrissy leaves."

"I have that feeling, too," her mother said. She looked down at her watch. "Goodness!" she said. "I did doze off. It's getting late. Weren't you and Tracy supposed to have one last night on the town this evening?"

"We were," Caroline said, "but she's got a cold, so she thought she'd better stay in tonight. I think I'll call and see how she's doing, though."

"Good idea. I'm going to go do a little work at my desk."

Caroline walked to the hall phone and dialed Tracy's number.

"Oh, Caroline, it's you," Tracy's mother said. "I don't know if Tracy will want to talk to you right now. She's pretty upset."

Upset with her? Caroline wondered. She hadn't even talked to Tracy since they'd canceled their plans that morning.

"Hello?" Tracy's voice, thick from the cold and cracking as if she were holding back tears, came over the line. "Cara?"

"Tracy? What's wrong?"

"Oh, Cara, I just got some awful news."

"Tracy, what is it?"

"Remember that I told you my mom took me to the doctor yesterday, just to be on the safe side?"

"Yes . . ."

"The doctor took a throat culture to make sure my sore throat wasn't strep," Tracy went on, barely holding back the tears. "Well, he called this evening with results from the lab. It wasn't strep at all, Cara."

"Well, that's good," Caroline said nervously.

"No, it's terrible," Tracy blurted. "I've got mononucleosis, Cara."

Caroline had to stop herself from laughing. "Don't you get that from kissing?" she asked.

"That's an old wives' tale." Tracy's heavy voice crackled over the line. "You get it from being overstressed and rundown. It happens a lot during periods like final exam week."

"Well, school's out now, Tracy. You can relax. You'll be better in no time, especially with all that fresh air up at camp—"

"Cara," Tracy cut in. "I don't think you understand. I've got mono. I'm contagious. I can't go to camp!"

"Oh, no," Caroline was speechless. "I'm so sorry, Tracy," she managed to say. "Can't you at least come up after you get better?"

A big sob echoed through the phone. "Mono takes about six weeks to recover from. By then it will be too late . . ."

"Oh, Tracy," Caroline mumbled. "That's terrible. Is there anything I can do? Maybe I should stay home and keep you company."

"Don't be crazy," Tracy said, sounding more like herself. "You have a job to do. You go and have a great time. Then you can tell me what to expect next year. Just promise to write me lots of letters."

"I will, Tracy," Caroline said. A new awful thought crept into her mind: Without Tracy, she'd be completely alone.

"I'm really sorry, Caroline," Tracy said, as if she had read her friend's mind. "It would have been such fun, the two of us together. Now you'll be alone in the woods, and I'll be reduced to watching soap operas all day."

"No, you won't," Caroline said. "For one thing, I'll make sure Chrissy comes to keep you company on a regular basis as soon as she gets back from her trip." She paused to listen to a noise at the front of the apartment. "Hey, I think I hear Chrissy coming up the stairs right now," she said. "Nobody else sounds like a herd of charging elephants . . . unless it *is* a herd of charging elephants. I'll put her on and she can say hello to you."

But Chrissy entered the apartment, slammed the front door behind her, and pushed through the hall past Caroline as if she weren't even there.

"Chrissy?" Caroline called after her. "Tracy's on the phone. She'd like to talk to you."

Chrissy opened the bedroom door, but did not appear.

"I don't want to talk to anyone right now," she called in a clenched voice. "All I want to do is go home." She burst into noisy tears as she slammed the bedroom door behind her.

Chapter 3

"Chrissy, what's wrong?" Caroline had promised Tracy she'd call back, then followed her cousin into the bedroom, where she was sprawled on the bed sobbing so violently that her whole body was shaking.

"What happened?" Caroline asked.

Chrissy raised her head. "It's Jeff," she said in between sobs.

"Is he hurt or something?"

"Worse than that!"

Caroline gasped. "Chrissy, you don't mean he's . . . Oh, Chrissy, he's not . . . he's not dead, is he?" She whispered the question, as if that might make it less horrible, somehow.

"He might as well be. I'm not going to see him again, ever."

18

Caroline didn't know whether to be relieved or furious. She decided to be relieved. By now, she had only herself to blame if she hadn't realized that Chrissy responded with equal force to every emotional crisis. "You two had a fight?" she asked, tiptoeing across to the bed and sitting down carefully beside her cousin.

Chrissy shook her head, her face still buried against the pillow.

"If you didn't have a fight," Caroline tried patiently, "why are you breaking up? Did he meet someone else?"

Chrissy sat up and shook her head again, so violently that tears sprayed onto Caroline's hand. "We definitely would have had a fight about that," she said. She wiped her eyes with her sleeve and took a deep breath. "He says he still really likes me," she managed to explain.

Caroline waited for more information. "But?" she asked at last. She reached out and hesitantly touched Chrissy's heaving back. "Do you want me to leave you alone for a while?"

Chrissy turned her head and gazed at Caroline with imploring eyes. "I want you to help me pack," she said.

"Well, OK, sure," Caroline mumbled. "Concentrating on your trip to the mountains should do you good."

Chrissy gave a big, shuddering sigh. "I'm not going to the mountains, Cara. I'm going home."

"Home?"

"I can't face it here any more," she said. "Knowing I won't see Jeff again. It's just too painful. And it's no use going to the mountains because I wouldn't enjoy it. I'd be too depressed to enjoy myself or even see the scenery. I'd probably step into the first crevasse on a glacier."

Caroline had to giggle at this. "There are no glaciers around Lake Tahoe, Chrissy. You'd be more likely to bump into a McDonalds!"

"I don't want to go, Cara. I want to go home."

"I still don't understand," Caroline said cautiously. "You said Jeff really likes you, but he doesn't want to see you again. That doesn't make sense."

Chrissy gave a half sigh, half sob. "It's not that he doesn't want to see me again, it's that he won't be around to see me again. He's leaving tomorrow, Cara. You remember I told you he was rehearsing with this new group? Well, they've been offered a chance to tour as the backup band to a big rock group. Jeff thinks it's too good to turn down."

"It is, isn't it?" Caroline said hesitantly. She did not want to make Chrissy cry again. "I mean, he loves his music, and this will be wonderful experience for him."

"I know," Chrissy agreed, "but he'll be away all summer. By the time he gets back, I'll be home in Iowa." She began to cry softly.

Caroline slid an arm around her shoulder. "Chrissy, you knew it had to end sometime. You weren't going to stay here, and he certainly wasn't going to follow you to Iowa."

"I know, and I thought I'd be able to deal with it, when the time came," Chrissy said quietly. "I guess I just hoped that he'd be more cut up about leaving. He seemed to think that saying good-bye was just one of those things."

"He wasn't even upset when you cried?"

Chrissy sat up straight. "I did not cry until after he'd gone," she said. "I have my pride, you know."

"You are an idiot," Caroline said fondly. "If he'd known how upset you were, maybe he could have told you how upset *he* really was."

"It doesn't even matter now," Chrissy said. "I won't see him again, so that's that."

"But you don't really want to go home right away, do you, Chrissy? The rest of us would miss you so much."

Chrissy shook her head sadly. "No, you wouldn't, at least not for long. Uncle Richard and Aunt Edith have their work, you and Tracy will be hundreds of miles away—"

"Tracy won't," Caroline interrupted. "Tracy has mono. She can't go to camp."

"Oh, poor Tracy," Chrissy said, her big blue eyes filling with tears again. "Everything seems to be going wrong for everyone, except you," she turned to Caroline.

"I don't mean to complain, but I'm not wild about going to a strange camp all alone," Caroline said. "I was really looking forward to going with Tracy, but now I'm not so sure. What if I make no friends? What if the campers don't even like me? And if no one likes me, who will I talk to when I'm feeling friendless and—" Caroline broke off abruptly as an idea occurred to her. Maybe she would have someone to talk to when she was lonely. She grinned at Chrissy.

"What's the matter?" Chrissy asked sharply. "Did the pillow make wrinkles on my face?"

"I was just thinking," Caroline stammered. "I have a brilliant idea."

"Yeah?"

"Chrissy, why don't you take Tracy's place at camp? Then you'd get to see the mountains, and you wouldn't be alone because I'd be with you, and you'd be so busy leading hikes and roasting pigs-in-a-blanket and weaving lanyards that you wouldn't have time to be depressed."

"I don't know," Chrissy said hesitantly. "For two whole months?"

"Come with me," Caroline pleaded. "It will be such fun. We'll eat home-cooked breakfasts every morning and have sing-alongs by the campfire in the evening, and we'll communicate with flashlight code at night in our cabins.

"Home-cooked breakfast?" Chrissy asked wistfully. Caroline knew she was weakening. The Kirbys seldom had anything more than toast and grapefruit in the morning.

"So you'll come?" she asked.

"I guess I'll give it a try," Chrissy said. "It beats sitting around here waiting for Jeff to come running home from his tour begging for forgiveness just so I can laugh at him."

"That's terrific, Chrissy," Caroline said, beaming at her. "I'll go and call Tracy, to find out if she's talked to the camp yet. Then you can call home. Then we'll grab the last of the praline ice cream and make ourselves huge grape soda floats, OK?"

"OK," Chrissy agreed, her face breaking into a big smile.

Chapter 4

"Is this what summer camps usually look like?" Chrissy muttered to Caroline.

They stood together at the edge of a clearing in a pine forest. The sweet scent of pines filled the air around them. The breeze sighed gently, and a blue jay screeched a warning overhead. But the beautiful, picture postcard scene disappeared when Caroline looked directly in front of her. Her gaze drifted from one bleak hut to the next. They were a uniform dark gray, and placed in a long row down the clearing.

"I don't know," Caroline admitted. "I've never been to a summer camp before."

"I was expecting something a little more . . ." Chrissy broke off, searching for the right word.

"Civilized?" Caroline filled in for her.

"Are you sure this is the right place?" Chrissy asked hopefully. "Your father didn't take the wrong turn when we left the freeway?"

"It's the right place," Caroline said. "There was even a sign down the track with an arrow saying Camp Catch-a-Rainbow."

Chrissy snorted. "That's a laugh to start with. The only thing we're liable to catch up here is a cold!"

Caroline shrugged her shoulders uneasily. "Maybe it will look better . . ."

"I know, when the happy campers arrive," Chrissy said.

"Come on," Caroline said. "Let's go find the camp director. This backpack weighs a ton."

She followed a trail of makeshift signs across the dusty area. Chrissy ran to catch up with her, half dragging her enormous bag.

"It looks so deserted," Chrissy said. "Where is everybody? Do you think it's like one of those horror movies where giant ants come and eat everybody?"

Caroline laughed. "If you see a giant ant, tell me," she said, "and we'll head back for the freeway. I think we might be early. The letter said between twelve and four, and it's only one."

"Which reminds me—I'm starving," Chrissy said. "Do you think they provide lunch before orientation?"

"We stopped for pancakes on the way up," Caroline reminded her.

"That was at least an hour ago," Chrissy complained.

"So what do we do now?" Chrissy asked.

"Go and find Mr. Ed, I guess," Caroline said hesitantly.

Chrissy grinned. "Wasn't that the name of a talking horse?" she asked. "I always wondered where he went when his show went off the air."

"Nothing would surprise me right now," Caroline said. "This place is giving me the creeps. Where is everybody?"

They wandered from one empty hut to the next. Even the hut that was marked Camp Director was locked and deserted. Caroline began to wonder whether Chrissy's joke about the giant ants was so farfetched after all. *Maybe we've got the wrong day,* she thought, *or the wrong month, or the wrong year!*

Her worrying was interrupted by sounds from the nearby hillside. Booted feet were tramping toward them, marching in step. Caroline froze. *We've stumbled into a military camp,* she thought.

"Oh, great, new recruits!" a voice yelled.

Caroline and Chrissy watched suspiciously as a group of young men marched to them in perfect synchronization. "Welcome to Camp Catch-a-Rainbow!" the lean, gray-haired man at the front of the line called. "Are you two more of my counselors?"

After breathing a long sigh of relief, Caroline mumbled an introduction for herself and Chrissy.

Mr. Ed extended a hand that nearly crushed Caroline's fingers. His face was deeply tanned and etched with lines, but his slim arms bulged with muscles. He looked horribly, terrifyingly fit!

"Glad to meet you both," he said heartily. "I've just taken the early arrivals on a little hike to show them the layout of the camp."

"Little hike up the sheer face of a cliff," one of the boys muttered, sinking gratefully to the steps of the nearest hut.

"I'll leave the introductions for later when we have our orientation meeting," Mr. Ed said, grinning at the girls. He checked his clipboard. "You have huts one and three. Go unpack and get settled in and we'll meet outside my hut at four to go over survival techniques and brush up on our outdoor skills. You boys come with me. There's a load of wood that needs bringing down for the campfire."

A couple of the boys gave Caroline and Chrissy a grin as they marched after the camp director.

"Talk about a fitness freak," Caroline muttered to Chrissy. "Did you see those muscles?"

"Yeah!" Chrissy said in an appreciative voice. "And that wavy blond hair! He wasn't half bad."

Caroline looked at her cousin in horror. "Mr. Ed?" she asked. "You thought Mr. Ed was cute?"

Chrissy looked at Caroline as if she was speaking Chinese. "Mr. Ed?" she shrieked. "Yuck! I was talking about that boy at the back of the line. The one in the pink muscle shirt. What a babe! It won't be so bad here after all."

"Boy, you sure recover fast," Caroline commented, shaking her head in disbelief. "Only twenty-four hours ago the world had ended. Now you're drooling over cute guys in muscle shirts."

"You said I needed something to help me get over Jeff," Chrissy said, her big blue eyes looking innocently at Caroline. "Well, getting over Jeff might not be as difficult as I thought."

"Do you mind if I take this hut?" Chrissy asked Caroline, pausing in front of hut three. "I can't drag my bag another step."

"I told you not to bring so much stuff," Caroline couldn't help saying.

"Sure, go ahead and take that hut. I'd rather have the one on the end. I can look out at the trees."

Caroline left Chrissy attempting to drag her oversize bag up the steps of her hut and walked down to the end of the line. Her hut was just as bleak inside. Six iron cots lined the wall. A dark brown army blanket lay folded at the bottom of the tattered foam mattress on each bed. There was one naked light bulb in the middle of the room. A small shelf for personal belongings stood beside each bed. The windows had no drapes, but were covered in mosquito screening.

Caroline chose the bed nearest the door, so she could stop anyone trying to sneak by after lights-out. She put her backpack on the bed and sat down. It was very hard. She stared across the bleak room, trying to fight back the rising panic. "What am I doing here?" she asked herself. "I

don't know anything about survival techniques
or outdoor skills." She shivered as she felt the
draft coming in under the door.

"It can't be that bad," she argued with herself.
"After all, it has a good reputation. Besides, camp
has to be fun too . . . I hope!" *At least Chrissy's
here,* she thought, *and I guess I'll get used to the
hard beds and the drafty door!*

She began to unpack her clothes, stacking
them neatly onto the shelves and hanging her
backpack on the hook above her bed. Then she
went to find Chrissy.

"Where am I going to put my things?" Chrissy
wailed as Caroline poked her head around the
door. "I've already filled those dumb shelves."

"Just leave the rest in your bag and tuck it
under your bed," Caroline said. "Although I bet
Mr. Ed will have bed inspection every morning,
and you'll get to do fifty push-ups if there's
anything on the floor."

Chrissy's eyes opened very wide. "You *are*
kidding, aren't you? You didn't mention stuff like
this when you told me how much fun camp
would be."

"Maybe we're worrying for nothing. Maybe
when the kids arrive it will turn into a regular
camp with softball games and swimming and
making key chains . . ."

"That reminds me," Chrissy said. "Isn't there
supposed to be a lake here?"

"I hope so!" Caroline agreed. "They definitely
talked about swimming and boating in the letters

I got. You finish unpacking and we'll go look for it."

"You might try and locate the bathrooms," Chrissy said. "It could be a matter of life and death in the middle of the night."

Caroline laughed uneasily. "I hadn't thought about that," she said.

"It was the very first thing *I* thought about," Chrissy said.

"I'll go check them out." Caroline turned toward the door. "I hope there are hot showers."

"You'd better just pray for running water," Chrissy said. "We might have to drag up buckets from the lake each morning."

"You sure know how to cheer a person up," Caroline said. The bathroom was about two huts away—a long thin building among the trees with signs saying Boys and Girls at either end. Caroline pushed open the door cautiously and saw a row of sinks, two showers, and three toilets. She turned on a faucet, and ice-cold water came trickling out. She waited patiently but the water remained an ice-cold trickle. She pushed open a toilet door and jumped back as a frightened bug scurried across the floor. Her heart beat fast as she saw it was an enormous hairy spider.

"Did you find the bathrooms?" Chrissy called as Caroline emerged hastily from the hut.

"Yes, and I don't think I'm going in there again all summer," she answered.

"Cold water?"

"And worse. A spider."

Chrissy started to laugh. "You ran away from a spider? Boy, are you in for trouble this summer. I hate to tell you this, but the great outdoors is full of spiders!"

"This was a big spider," Caroline said grouchily. She was still trembling. "Almost as big as my hand, I swear!"

Chrissy went on laughing easily. "Well, if that's the worst thing we have to fear up here, I guess I'll survive. When you grow up on a farm, you're used to bugs." She looked across at Caroline with a big grin. "You're not used to any of the wonders of nature, are you? Remember the time those chickens attacked you on our farm?" She started giggling even louder.

Caroline knew she wasn't the great-outdoors type. Why hadn't she realized that a summer camp would mean wrestling with bugs and beasts all day, every day? Of course, Chrissy would be fine. When they were in Iowa, Chrissy had handled pigs and cows and frogs and every sort of bug with the same casual attitude. But this camp was supposed to be Caroline's territory. She had found it; she had gotten hired to be a counselor. Chrissy was only along because she needed a place to go while her broken heart healed. Caroline was determined not to be shown up by Chrissy this time.

"Come on," Caroline said in what she hoped was a hearty, outdoorsy voice, "Let's go find the lake."

Chapter 5

The lake was just down the hill from the camp, down a sandy trail winding between giant boulders. It glistened with sparkling blue water as the girls glimpsed it through the trees. It was sheer beauty. "Wow!" Caroline and Chrissy said at the same time.

"I hope we have some free time every day," Caroline said. Her tension slipped away as she gazed out at the calm blue water. "I'd love to bring a book here and just sit."

"You'd better watch out for the spiders," Chrissy teased. "And don't forget the killer ants. They can strip a person to a skeleton in five seconds."

"Ha, ha," Caroline said, hoping she sounded more lighthearted than she felt. "We'll see what an outdoor expert you are, Chrissy, when Mr. Ed chooses you to shoot the rapids or build a rope bridge."

"Elementary, my dear Watson," Chrissy replied smoothly. "You forget that I've been camping with my family since I could walk. All this is old hat to me. The wilderness is my true home!"

"Ha!" Caroline snorted. "Wait until we meet our first rattlesnake."

"Rattlesnake?" Chrissy asked, her smile faltering.

"These hills are full of them," Caroline said. "And bears . . . have you ever faced a full-grown bear?"

"You're putting me on," Chrissy said, grinning again but not no broadly. "There're no bears around here."

"Wait until you meet a large furry object on your way to the bathroom at night," Caroline said. "And it growls at you . . ."

"Ha! I've dealt with hogs and bulls," Chrissy said bravely. "I bet I can deal with bears."

Caroline turned away to look at the lake. *She probably can*, she thought unhappily. *She can probably deal with anything. I'm the one who won't know what to do if I meet a snake or a bear.*

As they reached the shore of the lake they saw that there was a small, wooden jetty extending from a sandy beach area. A lone figure sat at the end of the jetty, feet dangling in the water.

Chrissy stopped and grabbed at Caroline. "It's

him," she whispered. "The cute guy. Take a look at him now and tell me if you don't think he's gorgeous."

The boy apparently had not heard them coming. He stared out across the lake. Caroline took in the sun-streaked hair, the dark tan, the sharp, masculine profile. The wind blew his bangs across his face. He automatically reached up to push them back. There was something about this scene that reminded Caroline of old-time sailing ships and rugged adventure.

"Don't you think he's cute?" Chrissy insisted.

Cute wasn't the word that was forming in Caroline's mind. She wanted to say that he was interesting, but she knew Chrissy would interpret it the wrong way. To her, when you said "interesting" you meant "boring."

She nodded to Chrissy. "Definitely cute," she whispered.

"Now at least I'll have an outside interest to keep me occupied," Chrissy said smugly.

"How do you know I might not want him myself?" Caroline asked.

"You?" Chrissy grinned again. "You don't go around falling for handsome hunks in muscle shirts. You stick to quiet, sensible people like good old Roger."

"Maybe I've decided to change," Caroline said.

"Well, tough luck," Chrissy said, patting Caroline on the shoulder. "I saw him first, and he's going to help take my mind off of Jeff."

"Maybe I want to take my mind off of Roger

and Luke," Caroline said. Normally she hated battling with Chrissy, but suddenly it seemed very important to her. At a time when she felt so insecure about her future, she wasn't going to let Chrissy walk all over her.

Chrissy looked at Caroline in surprise.

The boy on the jetty must have heard their voices. He abruptly turned around. Seeing them, he got slowly to his feet.

"Have you been sent to drag me back to camp?" he asked. He gave a little half smile that made him even more gorgeous, revealing perfect white teeth and little laugh lines at the corners of his eyes.

"We just came down to look at the lake," Chrissy said before Caroline could speak.

"You two are counselors, right?" he asked, jumping down from the jetty with an easy leap.

"Right," they both said this time.

"Sort of a dump, isn't it?" he asked. "And the camp director—I get the feeling he's going to be a slave driver." He glanced around as if he suspected Mr. Ed might be sneaking up on them, then his gaze settled on several canoes lined up on the sand. "He had me bring down these canoes, so I decided I'd take a few minutes off and check out the lake. It's bigger than I thought. I don't know how I'm supposed to rescue somebody on the far side."

"You're the lifeguard here?" Chrissy asked.

"One of them, I hope," he said. "It's a big lake! I'm also in charge of bunk number two."

"Oh, great, you're between us," Chrissy said.

The boy looked at Caroline as if he had just noticed her for the first time. "I hope neither of you snores," he said. Caroline felt the red creeping into her cheeks under his direct gaze. She was, as Chrissy had said, not used to boys like this—the tanned and muscled hunks who walked around school in bright patterned shorts, always accompanied by bouncy blonde girls.

He glanced at his watch. "I guess we'd better be getting back to the slave driver," he said. "Orientation at four." He continued to stare at Caroline. "By the way," he asked as they began walking, what's your name?" Just as Caroline was about to answer, Chrissy opened her mouth.

"I'm Chrissy," she said. "That's my cousin, Caroline."

"I'm Peter. Where are you from?"

"San Francisco," Chrissy and Caroline said at the same time. Caroline shot Chrissy an evil look and fought back a desire to tell Peter that Chrissy was really from Danbury, Iowa.

"I'm from L.A.," Peter said. "At least, Santa Monica. You know it? Good beaches. Great surf. You guys like surfing?"

"Chrissy does," Caroline said, glancing at her cousin. She could tell that Chrissy remembered her first visit to an ocean, when she had been knocked over by a big wave. She gave Caroline a warning glance. Caroline grinned, delighted that she finally had been able to score a point.

"Great," Peter said, turning to Chrissy. "Are

there good surfing beaches around San Francisco?"

"It's too cold for most people," Chrissy said hastily. "The famous fog, remember?"

"Oh, right," Peter nodded. "I couldn't live in the fog. I go crazy if I don't get to the beach every day. I don't know what I'm doing here, actually, except that I needed the money and wanted to get away for the summer. My stepfather's kids come out to visit. They're from some hick town in the Midwest. Talk about dumbos . . ."

Chrissy shot Caroline another warning look that said, "Mention that I'm from Iowa and you're dead!" Caroline grinned to herself. She was definitely winning this little war. Now she was on her toes again, ready to face anything. She smiled shyly as Peter's eye caught hers. He certainly was cute. There was no way she was going to just hand him over to Chrissy.

They reached the camp and paused by Caroline's hut.

"I guess I'll see you guys at orientation in a few minutes," Peter said. "I need to get a drink of water first. I suppose I'd better find out if the water is drinkable!"

He walked away across the campground. Caroline and Chrissy watched him go.

"What a babe," Chrissy murmured.

"And he seems nice, too," Caroline agreed, staring after him.

"You weren't serious, were you?" Chrissy asked.

"About what?"

"About being interested in him yourself? He really isn't your type."

"I might have decided to change my type."

"Come on, Cara," Chrissy pleaded. "Stop teasing."

"I'm not teasing, Chrissy," Caroline said. She hadn't really planned on becoming interested in anyone this summer, and she was not the type of person, as Chrissy had said, who chased boys. All her relationships with boys so far had happened by accident. She had never, in her life, set out to make a boy notice her and succeeded.

Then again, she had never faced the great outdoors before, either; and she'd never before been responsible for a group of small human beings. Life was rapidly filling with new experiences. Maybe getting a boy to notice her would be one of them.

"You mean you're really going after this guy?" Chrissy asked in surprise.

"Why not?"

A smile flickered across Chrissy's lips. "And you think you've got a chance?" she asked. "He's very cute, you know. I bet all the girl counselors will be after him."

"So? It will be more of a challenge that way."

"And then there's me," Chrissy said, tossing her hair back over her shoulders. "You think you can make him notice you while I'm around?"

Caroline knew her cousin was only teasing. The easy, open friendly smile remained on her face. As far as Chrissy was concerned, it was just a playful little challenge. But for once, Caroline was ready to take the challenge. If any guy were worth chasing, it would be someone like Peter— someone whose eyes twinkled with fun, someone so cute that all the girls would envy you when you walked by holding his hand.

"Wait and see, Chrissy," she said smoothly. "Just you wait and see. You'd be surprised what I can do when I put my mind to it."

Chapter 6

"Let's begin with the basics," Mr. Ed said, looking around the cirle at his counselors. "How about the Outdoor Code?"

Caroline glanced from one face to the next. Outdoor Code? She didn't even know there was one. Was it something you learned and recited like the Pledge of Allegiance?

"Elizabeth, you begin," Mr. Ed said, directing his attention to a stunningly beautiful girl who sat beside him. "You've all met Elizabeth, my niece, haven't you? She'll be your head counselor this year."

Caroline took in the peach-colored, skintight shorts, the matching halter that showed off a rich, deep tan, the perfect makeup, the little white sandals. Elizabeth gave a modest smile and tossed back her flipped, black curls with a red-tipped finger. She looked more like a model for a hair-spray commercial than a head counselor. *I bet* she *never crossed a rope bridge suspended by her teeth,* Caroline thought, feeling less nervous. *She looks as if she'd flip if she broke a fingernail.*

"Let me see, the Outdoor Code," Elizabeth drawled, looking around the group, her gaze lingering longer on the boys than the girls. "Always leave an area as you found it and take out everything you brought in. Only hike on marked trails—"

"Er, fine, Elizabeth," her uncle cut in before she could recite every wilderness rule single-handedly. "How about someone else going on. Let's move around the circle. Brandon?" He indicated the boy next to Elizabeth.

"Don't light fires without permission," Brandon said easily.

Mr. Ed's finger moved to the next boy. "Josh?"

"Always swim or hike with a buddy," he chimed.

"Peter?" He pointed at the gorgeous lifeguard.

"Tell someone where you are going?" Peter asked hesitantly.

Mon dieu, they do all know it like a pledge! Caroline thought in panic. She wondered how long the Outdoor Code was and if they would possibly run out before they got to her. *Anyway,* she thought with relief, *Chrissy is before me and she won't know what to say either.*

Mr. Ed's finger moved around the circle. Everyone seemed to have a suggestion to add until he reached Chrissy.

"How about you young lady?" Mr. Ed asked.

"Stay away from rattlesnakes and bears?" Chrissy asked. The group broke into noisy laughter.

"Sorry, I couldn't think of anything else," Chrissy said, laughing along with them.

"That's right," Mr. Ed agreed, much to Caroline's surprise. "We have just about covered everything on that. Now let's go on to first aid techniques."

Caroline managed to sit through the next half hour without saying a word, desperately trying to take in everything that was being said. With each new rule, she was more and more convinced that she was completely unprepared for her job. *I'll just have to stick with the other counselors all the time, and if anything happens, I'll holler for help,* she decided.

"Very good," Mr. Ed continued. "Let's break for chow, and then you have free time for a swim to cool off, if our lifeguard is agreeable?"

"I just wanted to check on one thing, sir," Peter began. "Am I the only lifeguard? It seems to me that it's going to be very hard to keep my eye on the entire lake. Especially if you have kids out in canoes."

"Don't worry, Peter, I'm here to help you. I'm a qualified lifeguard," Elizabeth's deep, cool voice floated across the circle. "I don't have a bunk of my own to keep an eye on, so I'll be pleased to give you a hand."

She gave him a long, steady smile. She looked just like a tiger who had sighted a tethered kid. Caroline glanced across at Chrissy, and Chrissy wrinkled her nose. Caroline giggled.

"And when we've had our swim, we'll meet informally around the campfire." Mr. Ed went on, seemingly unaware of any of the looks that had been exchanged between people in the circle. "Tomorrow morning we'll go on an orientation hike, and I'll show you which areas are off-limits to campers. Then we'll go through the day plan for the first week. I'll hand out assignments and camper lists—"

"And then we'll have breakfast," a voice muttered, breaking up the meeting with laughter.

Caroline and Chrissy left the group together.

"I think we've got competition," Caroline commented when they were safely far away from the rest of the counselors.

"Elizabeth, you mean?"

"Sure. Did you see the way she looked at him?"

"So?" Chrissy asked easily. "I'm not worried."

"But Chrissy, that girl is gorgeous. Everything about her is perfect. What's more sickening—she can obviously do everything without breaking her fingernails!"

"So? You're not looking at a little novice here, you know. I know about men. I've still got a few ideas up my sleeve," Chrissy said confidently. "It all comes down to finding ways to make a boy notice you. When Peter has gazed into my big, baby-blue eyes, he'll forget the name Elizabeth even exists!"

Caroline giggled. "I don't know how," she said. "From the look of that girl, she'll probably carry him off to the nearest cave."

"Men aren't always attracted to women who can do everything," Chrissy said firmly. "Girls like Elizabeth give boys big inferiority complexes. That's my big advantage: where I come from girls are encouraged to act helpless. We're trained to be shy and charming and wait for boys to come and protect us."

Caroline laughed loudly. "I remember watching you be shy and charming with your rival, Tammy what's-her-name. Does pushing her into a plate of blueberry pie fall into the category of shy, or is that more charming?"

"She asked for it," Chrissy said. "And that should prove to you that I'm willing to fight for the man I want. So watch out, both you and Elizabeth, because you're playing with fire!"

Caroline's giggles entirely convulsed her. She looked across helplessly at her cousin, who was still putting on her proud and haughty Wonder Woman look while trying to look sexy at the same time. Every time Chrissy half closed her eyes and fluttered her eyelashes Caroline giggled even harder.

"You just wait and see," Chrissy said, striding out ahead of her cousin." I bet I've got Peter eating out of my hand by morning!"

"I'll wait and see," Caroline gasped.

"I'll have you know you're looking at an experi-enced pro when it comes to attracting boys," Chrissy said, swinging her hips exaggeratedly as she walked.

Caroline spluttered with laughter. "Oh, Chrissy, come on," she said.

"OK, what about Hunter Bryce, what about Jeff?" Chrissy demanded. "You have to admit that those are—correction, were—two gorgeous guys!"

"Sure, I admit that," Caroline said. "But neither one of them fell for you because you wiggled your hips like that. Hunter noticed you because you were building a tower of old cans, which he mistook for art, and Jeff noticed you while you were tagging sea lions."

"Which just proves what I've been saying," Chrissy insisted.

"It does not," Caroline objected. "First you said that men were attracted to helpless girls, and now you say that Jeff liked you because you were tagging sea lions—not exactly what helpless girls do in their spare time."

"But I needed his help to subdue them," she said. "He got to show off his muscles and feel needed at the same time. Boys like that sort of stuff. You just watch, and I'll give you a lesson in attracting a guy. You might learn something—not in time to get Peter, unfortunately, but for future reference."

"You are a pain sometimes," Caroline muttered.

"I still think that if I had to bet on any of us, my money would go on Elizabeth."

They disappeared into their cabins to change. As Caroline slipped into her bathing suit, she realized clearly that starting the next morning, she would be changing in front of six little girls. *It's a good thing I've shared a room with Chrissy for a year,* she thought. *I would have freaked out at the thought of taking my clothes off in front of anyone before that. I remember I always changed in my sleeping bag at slumber parties!*

She wished she had a mirror to check the fit of the new maillot, but what she could see looked pretty good. *Black will be a great color on me when I get a good tan,* she thought. She slipped a sweatshirt over the suit and walked to join Chrissy.

"Are you ready yet?" she called, knocking on the door.

"Almost," Chrissy yelled back. "Come on in." Caroline walked inside.

"So how do I look?" Chrissy asked.

"You're wearing *that* to swim in the lake?" Caroline exclaimed. Chrissy had on three little triangles of white lace, held together by something like shoestrings.

"It's a swimsuit, isn't it?" she asked.

"But Chrissy, you bought that to sunbathe in, not to swim in. If you dive in, the whole thing will fall off!"

"So I don't know how to dive," Chrissy said,

"and I'll swim very gently. I think it will have the right effect."

"On Peter, you mean?" Caroline asked sharply.

"Well, I bet this is what the girls down in Santa Monica wear," Chrissy said. She slunk toward the doorway and down the steps, leaving Caroline to follow behind her, half hoping that the bikini would fall off as soon as Chrissy entered the water. *Serve her right, she is being so darned cocky today,* she thought.

Most of the boys were already swimming, looking up with loud whistles as the girls approached. Caroline blushed, although she knew the whistles were not aimed at her. She saw Peter out at his lifeguard's position at the edge of the dock. He didn't even notice them. He obviously took his duties very seriously, Caroline decided.

Elizabeth was sunning on the beach, perched on the side of one of the canoes, talking to another girl counselor.

"You'd better not wear that when the kids arrive," she said as Chrissy passed her. "You don't know what those eleven-year-old boys are like! When you've been here a few weeks you'll learn to dress for survival." She turned and laughed with the other girl, who nodded in agreement. "Remember Tommy Robins last year? That wretched kid. He put *two* frogs in my bed . . . "

The water was much colder than the girls expected. It felt icy cold like freshly melted snow. Caroline was a pretty strong swimmer and didn't want to look like a wimp getting into the water, so she strode straight out into it and broke into an easy freestyle stroke. After she had gotten over the initial shock, she found the water refreshing. She turned onto her back and moved out further into the lake, looking at the pink evening sky and the dark shadows on the cliffs above. A blue jay flew across the water and, higher up, a big bird of prey was circling. It was a very peaceful scene and Caroline felt herself relaxing completely.

Her daydreaming was interrupted by what sounded like a piercing cry. Alarmed, she turned over in time to see Chrissy, behind her, waving her arms frantically in the air.

"What is it?" she yelled.

"A cramp! I've got a cramp in my foot!" Chrissy was yelling. "Help, I'm drowning!"

"Hold on," Caroline called, swimming toward her.

"Not you, idiot!" Chrissy hissed under her breath. She rotated until she was directly facing Peter. "Help!" she called feebly. Caroline stopped paddling as Chrissy's plan became clear to her. She couldn't believe Chrissy would stoop that low for a boy.

"What's up?" Peter asked with only mild interest. Caroline smiled. Apparently, Peter was quite familiar with how low a girl would go for his attention.

"I've got a cramp. Help!" Chrissy called, still waving her arms around. "I can't move my foot! It hurts!"

"Massage it," Peter called back.

"Ow, it's really hurting. I can't move my leg at all," Chrissy shouted.

"Swim with the other one," Peter called back good-naturedly.

"Aren't you going to dive in and save me?" Chrissy demanded in a hurt voice.

A grin spread across Peter's face. "I figure anyone who can argue with me has enough strength to get to the shore. Besides, you can stand up there."

"Some lifeguard you are!" Chrissy yelled back. "I'm getting weaker. I think I'm drowning! Somebody help me!"

On the shore there was a faint splash. Suddenly a body broke the surface beside Chrissy. "Just relax and I'll have you to shore in no time at all," Elizabeth said soothingly. She began to swim with powerful strokes Chrissy pinned under her left arm, unable to move, unable to protest. Chrissy shot Caroline one despairing look as Elizabeth disappeared with her. Caroline was laughing so hard, she found it difficult to swim into shore behind them.

Chapter 7

"I think it was downright mean of him," Chrissy muttered as she walked beside Caroline back to the cabins. "What if I really did have a cramp? I might have drowned!"

"Chrissy, he knew you were faking," Caroline said, still unable to hide her amusement. "What drowning victim carries on a conversation? Besides, I bet he sees girls pull that trick all the time."

"Hhmmmph," Chrissy growled. "I thought I was very convincing! It was so cold in there that my legs really wouldn't move properly. I almost did have a cramp."

"Well, anyway, that's round one to Elizabeth," Caroline said.

"That girl is a big pain," Chrissy growled. "Did

you hear the way she lectured me after she almost drowned me towing me out? I told her she had my head under the water, and she said that was standard procedure to keep victims quiet!"

Caroline tried hard not to smile. After all, Chrissy had just had a shock. It could not have been pleasant being dragged out of the lake by Elizabeth on her first evening and having to persuade her very firmly not to begin artificial respiration or CPR—especially since Peter had turned around and was still watching with amusement.

"So much for the little-miss-helpless routine," Caroline said dryly. "I think you're going to have to come up with something more subtle than that if you want to make Peter notice you."

"Don't worry, I have alternative plans," Chrissy said. "At least he now knows who I am, and I guess he knows I'm interested. Boys like that. It flatters their ego."

They reached the cabins. Caroline shivered in the cool evening wind. "Gee, it gets cold here at night," she commented. "I hope those army blankets keep the wind out."

"If they don't, we can phone your folks to send up a couple of down bags," Chrissy suggested, wrapping her towel around her more protectively.

"We couldn't do that, Chrissy," Caroline said. "We have to set an example for our campers. The poor little things are going to feel the cold much more than we are." She stopped at the doorway, looking out across the deserted camp. The wind whipped around her damp legs, making her shiver, as much with nervousness as with cold. "It seems weird to think that they arrive tomorrow afternoon," she said. "Just think, this time tomorrow, we'll be responsible for five other people, all the time. We won't have any time to ourselves, and we'll have to keep our eyes open every minute in case they do something dumb."

"I intend to keep enough time free to chase Peter," Chrissy said.

"In which case we'd better hurry and change right now," Caroline commented. "If we don't get a move on, Elizabeth will already have lit the campfire single-handedly and probably have snared Peter in a lasso contest."

Chrissy giggled. "That's not such a bad idea," she said, her eyes lighting up hopefully. "A lasso contest. I used to be hot stuff with a rope, back in the good old 4-H days! Maybe I'll suggest that at the campfire tonight! I wonder what sexy dress I should wear. Too bad you didn't follow my advice and pack your white one with the low neck."

"Chrissy, it was totally wrong for a camp," Caroline said. "Besides, you know me. I don't like to stand out from the crowd."

"A guy can't notice you if he doesn't see you," Chrissy suggested, running up the steps to her own cabin. Caroline stomped up the steps into hers. It was dark now and the naked bulb exaggerated the bleakness of the huts. For the first time, Caroline realized that she was very far from home and stuck there for two whole months. *Thank heavens Chrissy is here, or I'd be so lonely,* she thought. *Although I could do without the way she's acting right now. She's carrying this catch-Peter routine a little far. Between Elizabeth and Chrissy, the poor boy barely has room to breath. At least he didn't fall for Chrissy's crazy drowning act! That proves he's not one of those mindless bums who's head is turned by an itsy-bitsy bikini and lots of blonde hair. Maybe he's really a quiet intellectual and there's some hope for me.*

Caroline paused to smile to herself as she slipped on her sweatshirt, jeans, and jacket. *Wouldn't that be something?* she asked herself, continuing her fantasy. Mr. Ed would send the two of them on some special mission. Away from the bustle of camp, they'd start to talk. Peter would be pleasantly surprised when he found out that Caroline was interesting and sensitive. "Those other girls come on so strong," he would say. "I felt really uneasy around them, but you, I can really talk to you." She imagined herself and Peter, sitting together, discussing things. Then she pictured Chrissy's and Elizabeth's faces when Peter and Caroline walked past them, hand in hand, involved in a deep conversation. Elizabeth would make a play for Peter's attention, but he'd look up in annoyance. "Not now, we're busy," he'd say, and Caroline would try hard to hide her smile.

It's not so crazy, she told herself hopefully. *He*

might just like a girl like me. After all, I am a good listener, and I am intelligent, and I'm not coming on strong. If only he would notice that I am quiet and mature and a good friend . . ."

She ran the brush through her ash-blonde hair. It was still wet and there was no way to dry it. She had not seen any outlets in the bathrooms or in the cabin. *I hope Chrissy wasn't intending to style her hair tonight,* she thought. *And what about Elizabeth? How will her fabulous hairstyle look when she can't use a hot brush and dryer? Pretty soon we'll all be equal, and that's when brains and personality will count.*

She felt more hopeful as she swept her hair back into a ponytail and put on a hint of blusher and mascara. As she came out of her front door she met Chrissy, running up the steps toward her, out of breath.

"Cara, come quickly," she whispered, pulling Caroline down the steps, toward the bathroom.

"What's wrong?"

"I was in the bathroom, brushing my hair, putting on makeup, and I heard this noise outside—a sort of growling snuffling noise. I peeked out, and there was this big old bear, coming out of the forest. I just ran as fast as I could and I left my purse in the bathroom. Come back with me and get it, please?"

Caroline swallowed hard. She didn't want Chrissy to know that she was not anxious to meet a bear close up. "Shouldn't we tell someone?" she asked.

"Just come with me and get my purse first, please," Chrissy said. "It's got all my money and makeup and my address book in it. If I leave it in there and something happens to it, I'll never survive two months here."

"*If* there really is a bear back there, we should get help."

"It sure sounds like a bear," Caroline agreed. "Let's find Mr. Ed."

"Go see for yourself," Chrissy pleaded. "It was a big black animal, and it was snuffling around the trees. What else could that be?"

"I can't risk anyone seeing me like this," Chrissy said. "My hair looks like a haystack, and I've got one set of black eyelashes and one blonde. Cara, help me get my stuff."

"I'll go take a look, but if I see or hear anything that resembles a bear, I'm not going farther than the edge of this building."

She walked reluctantly down the path between the cabins. The light was on in Peter's hut, and she glimpsed someone moving around. *At least someone will come if I yell for help,* she thought.

She reached the end of the cabin and very cautiously poked her nose around it. Nothing moved in the blackness beyond. *I bet Chrissy was imagining things,* she thought with relief, *or if she wasn't, I bet the bear just went back into the forest. If I get her purse for her, it will show her I'm not a complete scaredy cat when it comes to the outdoors!*

She started to cross the clearing to the bathrooms. She turned to the girl's bathroom. Inching her way, she stepped through the door. All quiet. A sigh of relief escaped from her lungs, and she took another step forward—and almost landed on a large black shape, huddled asleep. As she jumped back in horror, it rose up in front of her, with a low moaning growl. Caroline turned and fled.

"Peter!" she yelled, hammering on his door, "Come quick!"

The door opened and Peter, a towel around his waist, appeared. "What is it?" he asked irritably.

"There's a bear in the girl's bathroom!"

He gave a weary smile. "Is this another little joke? Are you girls going to make my life here a real pain all the time?"

"It's no joke," Caroline said. "I almost stepped on it as I went in the doorway. A big black bear. Come and see for yourself."

"OK," he said. "Wait till I pull some shorts on, though. Too bad I'm out of bear repellant!"

He shut the door and appeared seconds later. "Now where is this bear?" he asked. Caroline pushed him ahead of her. "You go first," she whispered. "I don't want to meet it again."

"Gee, thanks a lot," Peter commented dryly.

"You're used to this," Caroline pleaded.

"All you do is shoo it away," Peter said, turning back to glance at her as they crept between the buildings. "As soon as it heard our voices, it probably disappeared."

As he was talking, there was a rustling of

leaves and a black shape appeared out of the darkness, coming toward them. Caroline screamed and turned to run.

"The bear!" Caroline yelled. "Quick, run!"

"That's the bear?" Peter asked.

"That's it," Caroline shouted, grabbing at his arm. "It's coming after us."

"Very funny. Good joke," Peter said dryly. "Have we any more amusing things planned or can I go back to getting dressed? I'm pretty cold, you know."

Caroline stood there, trembling and confused. "What about the bear?" she asked.

Peter whistled, and a very large shaggy dog appeared. He turned to her, his eyes cold and angry. "Some bear, huh?"

"A dog?"

"But it was so big," Caroline stammered.

Peter looked at her more closely, his anger changing to amusement. "You mean you really didn't know that it was Mr. Ed's dog?" he asked.

She shook her head, wishing the ground would open up and swallow her. "I didn't know he had a dog," she said. "I wasn't expecting a dog . . ." *I was expecting a bear because Chrissy told me it was a bear,* she thought angrily. *Where is she while I am making a fool of myself?*

Peter laughed, shaking his head as he looked at her. "You might be in for a tough time here if you're going to freak out over stuff like this," he said. "And if your campers ever find out you're a scaredy-cat, heaven help you!" He began to pet the big, old dog, which had recovered from Caroline's scream and was now wagging his tail from all the attention.

At that moment Chrissy appeared, in a fresh blue denim skirt with a crisp white blouse and red bandana. "Oh, hi, here you are," she said brightly. "Ready to go to the campfire yet?"

"It wasn't a bear after all," Caroline said, looking at her coldly. "It was only a dog."

"Yes, I heard," Chrissy said with a big grin. "The walls of these cabins are very thin."

Caroline was torn between wanting to let Peter know that her cousin was the one who had started the bear scare and not wanting to make Chrissy look like a fool, even though she certainly deserved it. After all, nothing would be gained by trying to pass the blame over to Chrissy. And Caroline was still the one who yelled for help and grabbed at Peter's arm! She still looked like a fool, whether she shared the spotlight with Chrissy or not."

"Are you guys coming?" Chrissy asked again.

Caroline turned away. "You go ahead," she said. "I don't feel like a campfire just now."

"Are you sure?" Chrissy hesitated.

Caroline nodded. "Yes, I'm sure. Go on without me. I'll join you later, maybe. I need to calm my shattered nerves."

Peter turned back to her with a big smile. "Better lock your door in case Bigfoot's in the neighborhood tonight," he said.

"Very funny," Caroline growled. She turned and ran back into her cabin.

I don't know why I liked him at all, she thought. *He's totally conceited and obviously thinks he's wonderful. I hate that sort of boy. Chrissy can have him, if she can get him. Any boy who laughs at a girl when she is scared is not my type.*

She sank down on her cot and ran her fingers over the rough, brown surface of the blankets. As she stared into the black sky, dotted with twinkling stars, her thoughts drifted, as they often did, back to Luke, the boy she'd fallen in love with when she visited Chrissy's home in Iowa. If she had screamed for help, Luke would have come running instantly. He would have swept her up in his strong arms and carried her away from the big old bear. She shivered as she almost felt, physically, the touch of his arms around her. *Will I ever get over him, ever?* she wondered. *Will there ever be another boy in my life who makes me feel the way Luke did? Sometimes I'm really scared that I'll never feel anything for anyone again.*

She conjured up a mental picture of Peter in her mind. *Super cute, definitely, but I don't think I was ever truly interested in him—except to annoy Chrissy because she was acting so superior.*

After hanging a towel over the window, she undressed slowly, then climbed into bed. She toyed with the idea of writing to Tracy, as she had promised to do, but the whole first day seemed to have consisted entirely of a chapter of accidents. *I'll wait until my campers arrive tomorrow and tell her about them,* she thought. *I do hope they like me and that we get along.*

A burst of laughter floated in from the campfire. *Maybe I was dumb not to have gone,* she thought. *I hope the others don't think I'm a snob or something, but I didn't want to be there when Peter told them all about the bear! He's probably told them and they all think I'm a total wimp.*

She lay back, unable to ignore the slightly unpleasant, damp smell of her pillow and how different it was from the gentle softness of her own bed at home. Her feet felt cold and damp. She wondered if she'd ever be warm enough to fall asleep.

Chrissy's at the campfire, fitting in with everyone else, she thought. *Nothing fazes Chrissy. I bet she wasn't even embarrassed that Elizabeth rescued her. She was only mad that it wasn't Peter. I wish I could be more like Chrissy and not care what people think of me.*

Her thoughts were interrupted by a tapping on her door.

"Cara, are you asleep?" Chrissy's voice came through the crack.

"No, come on in," Caroline called back.

Chrissy shut the door quietly behind her.

"So how was the campfire. Did everyone laugh about the bear?"

"Peter didn't mention it," Chrissy said. "Mostly, everyone was just telling a little about themselves, where they're from, what they like . . ."

"And what is everyone like?" Caroline asked.

Chrissy shrugged her shoulders. "Everyone's pretty ordinary, really," she said. "Except Elizabeth, of course. She's done everything and been everywhere. Did you know that her father climbs in the Himalayas? She told us at least a dozen times!"

There was something about Chrissy's manner that made Caroline uneasy. She had lived with her cousin long enough to know that there was something else on her mind.

"Is something wrong, Chrissy?" she asked. "Did you see Peter and Elizabeth together? I take it she got her claws into him the moment she saw him again."

Chrissy nodded. "They sat together," she said. "Very close."

"I'd forgot about it if I were you," Caroline said. "He may be cute, but if he falls for Elizabeth instead of one of us, how great can he be? Besides, he laughed at me when I was scared."

"Cara," Chrissy interrupted. "It's not Peter. I still think I have as good a chance as anyone with him. It's something else. I think I just did something dumb."

Caroline sat upright. A cold chill crept up her spine. *This is all too familiar,* she thought. "Like what?" she asked.

"Well . . ." Chrissy paused. "When we were all

telling about ourselves," Chrissy said, toying with the iron bed frame, "I just happened to mention that we were both in college."

Chapter 8

Caroline stared at her cousin, open-mouthed. She couldn't believe what she was hearing. "Chrissy, you didn't—"

Chrissy hung her head like a little girl who has been caught at the cookie jar.

"Christina Madden, what on earth made you do a crazy thing like that?" Caroline shrieked.

Chrissy looked around. "Keep your voice down! You can hear everything through these walls," she said. "Do you want the others to hear?"

"They're going to find out sooner or later," Caroline said firmly. "Now we'll never fit in!"

Chrissy grabbed at Caroline's arm. "But Cara, that's why I did it," she said. "Because we both did dumb things today, and I didn't want them all to look down on us."

"But why say we were in college?" Caroline demanded. "Isn't that pretty dumb?"

"I only said it because everyone else was," Chrissy said. "We went around the circle and everyone was saying how they were premed at Stanford and political science majors at UCLA and Cal Poly and I just imagined their faces when I said we were little high school seniors. I didn't want them to think we were beneath them!"

The frown did not leave Caroline's forehead. "And may I ask, which college I am supposed to be attending?"

Chrissy looked even more embarrassed. "Berkeley," she stammered.

"Berkeley? Chrissy, do you know that Berkeley only takes four point zeros? That makes us total brains. Couldn't you at least have said something harmless like San Francisco State?"

"I was caught off guard, and I knew that your parents went to Berkeley, so I figured you'd know a bit about it," Chrissy said. "Besides, you've taken me there, so we both know about the clock tower and Telegraph Avenue. It's also big enough so that we couldn't know everybody!"

Caroline sank back onto her pillow with a big sigh. "I don't know what I'm going to do with you, Chrissy," she said. "It's bound to come out that we're frauds. We don't know anything about life at Berkeley."

"We know about the clock tower," Chrissy

insisted. "We know there's a neat hamburger place across from the campus, because we ate there. Besides, I said we live at home. We commute daily."

"And do we have a major?" Caroline asked.

"I said you were an art major," Chrissy said. "You know tons about that."

"I hope you didn't say you were in art too," Caroline said dryly. "You've only just learned a Van Dyk from a Donald Duck!"

"Ha, ha," Chrissy said, shooting a withering look at Caroline. "I am a drama major." Chrissy added in a mock British accent. "I know how to be dramatic!"

Caroline giggled. "Your performance as the drowning victim isn't going to win you an Oscar."

"Oh, shut up," Chrissy said irritably. "And stop putting me down all the time. I did it for you as well as for me. You wanted to get along well with the other counselors. You sure could use someone to make you finally forget about Luke. I was getting my hopes up when you started acting so interested in Peter. I was ready to sacrifice my feelings to help you get over your great Love. So don't keep on bugging me. Do you think you'd really have enjoyed being stuck up here for two months with everyone else talking about college and ignoring us because we're only children?"

Caroline shrugged her shoulders uneasily. "But it's lying, Chrissy. You know I hate lying."

"So do I. But I also hate being left out of things. It's the only way one of us will ever have a chance with Peter. You know very well that a guy from UCLA wouldn't look twice at a kid from Maxwell High!"

"I don't care. You can have him," Caroline said. He really embarrassed me about the bear."

"You mean you're not interested in him any more?" Chrissy asked, her face beaming.

"That's right. You can fight it out with Elizabeth. He's not my type."

"I guess you got out of the kitchen because you couldn't stand the heat, huh?" Chrissy asked, somehwat smugly.

"What's that supposed to mean?"

"That you recognized the competition was too strong for you!"

"No way," Caroline said. "I just realized that it wasn't worth competing or lying for."

"Not even for the most gorgeous body this side of the Rockies?"

"Not even," Caroline replied. "Now, if you'll excuse me, I'm kind of tired. It's been an exhausting day."

Chrissy snorted. "If you think today was exhausting, you wait until the campers arrive tomorrow."

Caroline propped herself up on her elbow again. "Don't you start," she warned. "You are already beginning to sound just like Peter and Elizabeth—giving me smug warnings because they think they are such experts at everything. Well, you guys better look out! You might know how to climb trees and pick up spiders, but that still doesn't guarantee that you'll get along with your campers better than I will. Now good night!" Caroline pulled the covers over her head until she heard the cabin door slam behind Chrissy.

In spite of her exhaustion, Caroline had an almost sleepless night. The unfamiliar cabin, the damp coldness of the lumpy bed, the strange night rustlings and whistlings outside combined with the anxiety about having to pretend to be a college student kept her awake. As much as she hated what Chrissy had done, she had to play along, or they would both look like complete fools. She was stuck with being a Berkeley student whether she liked it or not.

The next morning she slipped into the breakfast line with Chrissy, hoping to stay invisible for as long as possible. Food was served in a little hut behind Mr. Ed's cabin and was eaten at long tables. The chilly morning air came in through the open windows. Beyond them, the grass and wild flowers sparkled with dew. Elizabeth, naturally, was at the front of the mess line, looking as if she had just stepped out of a fashion magazine.

"I bet she has her own personal outlet in her cabin!" Caroline whispered to Chrissy, "and her own personal hair stylist!"

"That's what you get for being the niece of the owner," Chrissy whispered back.

There were two girls at the front of the line with Elizabeth, tough-looking girls in short shorts and big hiking boots. They were talking and laughing like old friends. Behind them was a group of four boys who seemed to know each other from the year before.

I'd really love to be up here in a little cabin on my own, Caroline thought wistfully as she listened to the noisy laughter further up the line. *Or with some of my good friends. That way I could really enjoy these surroundings. Now I have to watch every word I say and keep an eye on five little kids. I won't even have time to notice the beautiful scenery!*

As she reached the food table, she shuddered at the thought of eating greasy pancakes and sausages for two months. She filled her bowl with cornflakes instead.

"Is that a Berkeley breakfast?" one of the boys quipped as he sat down beside her uninvited. "No wonder they can never beat Stanford in football."

"I'm just not a breakfast person," Caroline muttered, feeling her cheeks turning stupidly pink. Surely college students didn't blush, did they? Chrissy slid into the seat beside her, her own plate piled high with food.

"They're planning to use me as quarterback next year," she said, grinning. "I'm their secret weapon, so don't tell anybody."

The boys at the table laughed loudly.

"I think I'll try out for football then, the tall sandy-haired boy called Brandon quipped. "I wouldn't mind tackling you!"

"You wouldn't find it as easy as you think,"

Chrissy added, attacking her pancakes.

"We'll have to set up a football game on the beach and find out," Brandon said. The other boys nodded in agreement. Caroline munched cornflakes in silence. How come Chrissy was always so cool? She didn't hesitate to trade jokes or insults with strangers. When she had first arrived in California, Caroline thought she was a big flirt. Now she knew that Chrissy was just naturally friendly and outgoing, and she envied her for it. *If only I could just have her confidence. To be able to talk to people I don't know without planning out what I am going to say first,* she thought. *The boys all seem very friendly, and I'm sure I could have a great time here if I weren't so self-conscious.*

Mr. Ed appeared with his huge dog at his side just as they were finishing breakfast. "Ready to start work?" he asked, ultracheerfully. "Days begin early at camp. I don't want anyone over-sleeping, understood? Anyone caught in bed after the wake-up bell will be carried down and thrown in the lake!"

The boys laughed noisily at this. Caroline was glad that Chrissy had turned her into an early riser. *A year ago I would have found it impossible to get up at seven,* she thought, *but living with Chrissy I feel lazy if I'm not up at the crack of dawn.*

She got up and reached for Chrissy's plate.

"I'm not done yet," Chrissy complained. "There's still some syrup I want to mop up."

"Mr. Ed will probably make you run laps around the lake if you're not ready to leave when he is," Caroline said sweetly. "And Peter is already finished also."

Chrissy pushed her plate away and got up. She followed Caroline's gaze to Peter, who was emptying his plate. As they watched Peter, Elizabeth sneaked up behind him and placed her hands over his eyes. The sight of her confident smile was too much for Chrissy. She turned away suddenly.

"I've just decided," she said. "I'm not suitably dressed for this hike. Be back in a moment. Don't leave without me."

She ran back to her cabin, only to appear a few moments later in a peacock-blue halter, tiny white shorts, and dainty white-heeled sandals. Her hair was pulled across to one side in a ponytail, and her eyelashes were heavily mascaraed.

Caroline looked at her. She was speechless.

"I've decided to fight fire with fire," Chrissy said. "Elizabeth is winning by coming on strong and looking sexy, so I've decided to come on even stronger."

"Chrissy!" Caroline warned under her breath, but Chrissy just laughed. "You can now watch a master at work," she said.

She sidled across to Peter, who had managed to free himself from Elizabeth's hands.

"All ready for the hike?" she asked in a low,

sexy voice that made Caroline choke as she suppressed a giggle.

Peter stared at Chrissy. "Are you intending to hike in that?" he asked.

"Is something wrong with it?" Chrissy asked smoothly.

Peter's eyes looked her up and down. "Nothing's wrong with it," he said with a big grin. "But it doesn't look as if it will stand up to the type of hiking Mr. Ed has in mind."

"Oh, I'm used to hiking," Chrissy said confidently. "My family and I, we always walk for miles. I was born and brought up in the great outdoors."

"Minus the swimming part?" Peter asked.

"Cramps can happen to anybody," Chrissy said. "Even Olympic swimmers get cramps."

"Sure," Peter said, grinning at her before he turned away.

"See, it's working already," Chrissy whispered as she moved back to Caroline. "Did you see the way he smiled at me?"

"It was more of a grin, Chrissy," Caroline said. "He was laughing at you."

"He was not. It was definitely a big, friendly smile," Chrissy said.

"If you say so," Caroline replied while sitting to lace her sneakers.

Mr. Ed appeared, blowing a whistle that set his dog barking. Elizabeth showed up behind him, this time wearing what looked like an entire safari outfit complete with hiking boots. She had livened up the khaki with a brilliant orange scarf around her neck, still looking as gorgeous as ever.

"You don't intend to hike in that outfit?" she asked Chrissy.

"Why not?" Chrissy asked.

"Because, my dear, you won't get ten yards without being bitten and scratched to pieces."

"I'll survive," Chrissy said, smiling sweetly.

"Well, don't say I didn't warn you," Elizabeth said, turning away.

"She's jealous," Chrissy said with an excited grin to Caroline. "Did you see her face? For once, I look better than she does!"

As much as she hated to admit it, Caroline knew that Elizabeth was right.

The hike began, almost straight up the face of the nearest mountain. The trail zigzagged back and forth relentlessly, and the group fell strangely silent as they all fought for breath. Only Elizabeth's deep, sexy voice could be heard, carrying on a normal conversation with her uncle. The counselors reached the top of the ridge and had a breathtaking view of the snow-capped Sierra peaks in one direction and gentle blue foothills falling away toward the Pacific in the other. Caroline took deep breaths, her eyes feasting on the view. Chrissy slapped at mosquitos.

Mr. Ed pointed out the layout of the camp below them, showing them trails to other lakes and areas of rockslides and steep cliffs that were to be avoided. He took them along the top of the ridge on a gentle trail that wound between trees. Caroline noted that Chrissy was making an effort to draw level with Peter. As she went to follow Chrissy, someone tapped her on the shoulder.

"You're the one who goes to Berkeley, right?" a voice asked. Caroline turned to see a skinny little guy with spiked hair and glasses had moved up beside her. She longed to deny it, but couldn't. The little guy beamed at her. "I'm there too. Howard Rose, computer science. You have any computer science classes at all?"

Caroline hastily shook her head.

"Oh, but you should! They're great," Howard said, peering into her face. "They have them for beginners, you know. You come over to the lab next fall and I'll be happy to show you a thing or two. I'll fix you up with a real user-friendly model."

Caroline had a horrible vision of a blind date with a computer. She peered hopefully at Chrissy's back, willing her cousin to turn around and rescue her. Just as she mentioned politely that she wasn't really interested in computers, Howard launched into a long speech on computer art and how it could help her art training. She listened halfheartedly, noting that Chrissy was walking beside Peter and wishing that she could find a way to escape Howard.

Finally, the path mercifully narrowed, and there was only room to walk single file. Caroline fell into step behind Chrissy. Chrissy was no longer striding out like an experienced hiker.

"I can't keep this up much longer," she whispered to Caroline. "My feet are killing me! And don't say that you warned me," she added quickly. "At least I got to talk to Peter, so it was worth it."

The trail broadened out and they started downhill. Chrissy sat on a rock and took off her shoes.

"What's up?" Peter asked, looking back at her.

"Only blisters the size of dinner plates," Chrissy called back.

"Those aren't exactly hiking shoes," Peter commented.

"So I haven't had a chance to pick up army boots, like some of the girls here," Chrissy said.

"I wouldn't like to be your feet should you meet a snake," Peter said with a grin. He fell into step beside Caroline as Chrissy staggered to her feet again.

"Are you two sisters?" he asked with an amused smile.

"No, cousins," Caroline said.

"Oh, same family," he said, nodding. "Well, you sure aren't the outdoorsy type—hiking in itsy-bitsy sandals and running away from imaginary bears!"

Caroline gave him a withering look that made him chuckle.

"Actually, I understand about the bear now," he said. "You're from Berkeley, right? You're bound to have an obsession with bears."

Caroline's thoughts raced until she remembered, "Oh, you mean the Cal mascot is a bear?"

"Right."

"In which case you should be equally obsessed," she returned.

"How come?" He looked puzzled.

"Isn't a Bruin the same as a bear?" she asked. "You do go to UCLA, don't you?"

"Yeah," he said, "Oh sure ... Bruins. That's UCLA all right."

They walked a few paces in silence.

"So, um, what's your major?" Caroline asked. A simple, straightforward question.

"Er ... I haven't decided yet," he said. "I'm not sure what I want to do with my life."

"Me neither," Caroline said.

"I thought you were into art?"

"I still don't know what I want to do with my life," Caroline answered truthfully. "So what sort of courses are you taking?"

"Me?" Peter asked. "You know, general sort of things." He turned to look back at Chrissy.

"Do you think your cousin will make it home in those shoes?" he asked. "Or is she expecting one of us strong guys to carry her?"

"Don't underestimate Chrissy," Caroline said, watching her cousin striding out with a fierce look of concentration on her face. "She's tougher than she looks. She might end up carrying you."

Peter laughed warmly, and for a moment he seemed very human and appealing to Caroline. She could certainly see how a person could fall for him very easily—the way those blue eyes sparkled when he was amused. . . . She shut off the thought.

Chrissy caught up with them again as the trail crossed above the campsite.

"Hey, look, I've just seen a shortcut back to camp," she announced. "Why don't we just cut down here through these bushes and we'll come out right behind the eating area."

Peter turned to look at her in horror. "You don't seriously want to go down that slope?" he asked.

"Why not? It's not too steep," Chrissy said.

"Haven't you noticed that it's also wall-to-wall poison oak?" Peter asked.

"Poison oak? Is that what that is?" Chrissy asked innocently.

Peter laughed loudly. "Is that what that is?" he mimicked. "My god, you'd be sorry tomorrow if you went down there."

Elizabeth turned to see what the laughter was about, and dropped back to him.

"What's so funny?" she asked, slipping an arm through his. He was confused momentarily.

"Oh, just something Chrissy said," he stammered.

"Tell. I love a good joke," Elizabeth said, gazing up at him in a good imitation of an adoring look.

"Oh, she just suggested taking a shortcut down that hill," he said.

Elizabeth looked horrified and then roared with laughter.

"I can tell somebody was never a little Girl Scout," she said to Chrissy. She turned back to the

group with an expansive gesture: "In case anybody else doesn't know—this is poison oak!
Don't brush against it, don't even use the dead
wood for camp fires or you'll be very miserable
indeed!"

With that command she pranced back to the
front of the line. Peter fell into step again beside
Chrissy and Caroline.

"Well, how was I to know?" Chrissy mumbled
to Caroline. "You might have warned me."

"I wasn't a little Girl Scout either," she giggled,
mimicking Elizabeth's voice.

"Where have you been all your life?" Peter
asked with a grin. "Don't they teach you anything at Berkeley?"

"Back where I come from we don't have poison
oak," Chrissy exclaimed.

"They don't have poison oak in the Bay area?"
Peter asked. "What about all those hills behind
Berkeley? I know they've got to be full of poison
oak."

"What I meant was . . . " Chrissy stammered.

"She means that she's been a city person until
now," Caroline said hastily.

"I thought you said you'd done a lot of hiking,"
Peter added, looking at both of them suspiciously.

"I have," Chrissy said, "but not—"

"Not in the country. City hiking, that's what
she's done. She hikes for miles up and down the
hills of San Francisco," Caroline stated, "but she's

kept away from the area outside the city because of her allergies."

Peter nodded. "Somehow I get the feeling that you are not going to survive here for two months," he said seriously. "If the bears and snakes don't get you, the poison oak will!"

"Do you have to put people down all the time?" Caroline asked, fighting to control her growing anger. "Not everybody is an expert like you, you know. Just because Chrissy and I haven't had too much experience in outdoor survival does not make us morons! Get into a discussion on music or art with us, or even marine mammals for that matter, and you might find out that you don't know everything in the world!"

"Hey," Peter said, looking distinctly embarrassed at Caroline's outburst. "I didn't intend to . . . I mean it was only . . . I was only joking, you know."

With that he increased his pace to catch up with Elizabeth at the head of the line.

"Now do you see what I mean?" Caroline asked. "He is always putting you down, Chrissy. He thinks he's so wonderful!"

Chrissy watched his back as he headed down the trail with long, easy strides.

"That's the problem, Cara," Chrissy said with a big sigh. "He is!"

Chapter 9

At two o'clock that afternoon two yellow schoolbusses bumped and lurched their way into camp, belching out black fumes and leaving behind them a yellow haze of dust that hung in the still air. When the engines were switched off, there was complete silence. The doors opened, and, one by one, the campers climbed down, blinking in the strong sunlight and looking around with interest. There was no pushing or shoving, as if all of them had been warned to be on their best behavior. Caroline couldn't believe how small and helpless they looked. She was filled with a warm glow. *They all look scared stiff,* she thought. *I bet it's the first time away from home for most of them. I'll be able to look after them and make them feel happy here.*

Mr. Ed stepped forward and gave them a welcoming speech. It was clear to Caroline that most of the kids weren't listening. They were still looking around suspiciously, and in some she could see a glimmer of mischief waiting to explode. They eyed the campgrounds looking for the lake and wondering if the huts were really as uncomfortable as they looked. Mr. Ed finished his speech and introduced the counselors. "When your name is called, go to your counselor. Your counselor will be responsible for you for the whole time you are here."

The first counselor in line began to call off names from his list of boys in the Cougar cabin. Little boys swaggered across to him, each one trying to look tough and cool. Chrissy was assigned five tough-looking little girls for her cabin of Sharks. Somehow they looked even more aggressive and capable than the boys. Caroline's turn arrived, and she began to call off the names of the girls in her Barracuda cabin: Samantha Hastings, Francesca Martini, Rachel Howe, Kendall Rothmann, Jodi Thomas.

Five little girls came forward, looking up at her shyly. Her heart warmed to them instantly—cute, lovable little girls. Perfect campers.

"I'm Caroline and I'm your counselor," she said brightly, giving each of them an encouraging smile. "Let's get to know each other." She pointed at a scrawny girl who was staring at her with big, fearful eyes. "What's your name?"

"I'm Rachel," the little girl said. "And I didn't want to come here."

Caroline tried to keep the big smile going. "I'm sure you're going to have a great time," she said. "And who are you?" She turned to the next girl with a mass of black curls, wearing faded denim overalls. "Kendall," the girl said, "and I didn't want to come here either!"

Caroline swallowed hard. "Did any of you want to come here?" she asked.

"I did," a freckle-faced kid in torn jeans, wearing a baseball cap replied. "I'm Sam, short for Samantha."

"I'm Jodi—that's with an I not a Y—and I'm nearly twelve, old enough to take care of myself."

Caroline took in the low neck and the tight white pants and wondered if there might be trouble with this one. She smiled at Jodi and turned to the last girl, a serious-looking redhead. "And you are?"

The girl looked at her witheringly. "Francesca, the only name left."

Caroline's lips were beginning to ache from smiling so hard. "OK, gang," she said. "Grab your stuff and let's go to our cabin."

"Can you help me with mine?" Kendall, asked.

Caroline smiled at her. "Sure I can, which is yours?"

"This stuff here," she replied, pointing at a large mound of luggage. Caroline's eyes opened very wide. "All this?" she asked. "I thought you were told to bring one small suitcase each."

"But I couldn't get all my stuff in one small suitcase," the girl said. "I'm going to be here for four whole weeks, you know. A person needs to change clothes."

"I don't know where we're going to put it all," Caroline gasped, staggering under the weight of the trunk she had just lifted.

"Need some help?" Peter called out as he walked by with his boys.

"No, thank you. I can manage," Caroline said frostily. She gritted her teeth and managed to stagger up the steps of their cabin with the trunk. The girls followed her.

"Uggh, what a dump!"

"Where do I sleep?"

"There's no curtain on the window!"

Comments echoed behind Caroline as she lowered the trunk onto the nearest bunk.

"I don't want to sleep there," Kendall said in a not-at-all helpless voice. "I'll be too cold under the window."

"Someone's got to sleep there," Caroline said.

Kendall looked around the room. "I'll sleep there," she said, pointing at Caroline's bunk. "That way I can be first one out in case of a bear attack!"

"Bears!" Rachel shrieked. "I knew it. We're all going to be eaten alive."

"There are no bears here," Caroline said firmly, "And that's my bunk, Kendall. Choose another."

Kendall looked around the room. "They're all taken now," she said, "and I can't sleep under the window. You change with me," she said, pointing at Rachel.

Rachel's huge eyes opened even wider. "I can't sleep under a window! What if a wild animal crawled in? He'd get me first!"

"Well, I don't want to sleep under the window," Kendall whined.

"For pete's sake, I'll sleep on the crummy bed then," Sam said, pushing Kendall out of the way and dumping her own backpack on the bed.

"Anybody want to see a spider weaving a web?" Francesca asked dryly.

"Spiders!" Rachel screamed. "We have to sleep with spiders!"

"Ooohhh," Rachel wailed. Caroline stepped in hastily. "There is nothing to worry about, Rachel." She couldn't admit that she didn't like spiders either! "Now, please get your things unpacked so we can all meet at the campfire circle in half an hour."

The girls began to put their items on the shelves, chattering away like a bunch of magpies.

Later that afternoon when Caroline had some free time, she sat beside Chrissy on a large warm rock, writing her first letter to Tracy.

"It was not what I expected," Caroline wrote. "I expected helpless little kids and I got miniature adults. Instead of being assigned the Guppies, I got the Barracudas. They live up to their name! This job isn't going to be as easy as I thought."

She stopped writing and paused to look across

the peaceful lake. Chrissy was lying back, eyes closed, sunbathing. Some of the boys were playing Frisbee in the clearing, and there were screams and giggles from a group of the older girl campers as Peter walked past wearing his lifeguard T-shirt. Caroline chewed on her pen. "The counselors here are pretty nice, most of them," she wrote, "and we're all getting along fine." She stared down at the words she had written. She wanted to tell Tracy about Peter, how both she and Chrissy had a crush on him, but she didn't know where to begin. *Maybe I'll tell her about Elizabeth* she thought, but she couldn't think of the right words to describe supergirl.

Below her on the rock Chrissy stirred and opened her eyes.

"I must have nodded off to sleep," she murmured. "What time is it?"

"Nearly four-thirty."

Chrissy sat up and groaned. "I ache all over," she said. "My mosquito bites are throbbing, my blisters are throbbing, my scratches are throbbing." She examined her legs and feet and gave a sigh. "You know the first-aid kit that's supposed to last through the summer? I think I used it all up!" she said with a small giggle.

"First you try to drown," Caroline said, "Now this. Maybe next time you'll try to jump off a cliff to get Peter's attention."

"I'm not giving up, you know," Chrissy said. "I think he's a teeny little bit interested, don't you."

Caroline was about to add, "Only as an object of curiosity," but spared her cousin's feelings and said instead, "I think you'll have to lose Elizabeth in a deep canyon first. She's a smooth operator, and she's very determined."

"The deep canyon can be arranged," Chrissy said. "We saw a pretty spectacular drop this morning. One little push. . . ." She grinned and shrugged her shoulders. "Nah, knowing her, she'd grab onto a bush halfway down with one hand and vault back up again." She adjusted a Band-Aid on her toe. "It must be time for evening swim soon. Peter should be going down there any moment."

"He just went," Caroline said.

Chrissy jumped up. "Why didn't you wake me!" she wailed. "Now I'll have to rush and change."

"Chrissy!" Caroline pleaded. "Take it easy, will you? You're taking this too far."

"Just because I didn't quit at the first sign of competition," Chrissy said haughtily.

"I did not quit because of competition," Caroline said. "I quit when I found out that his personality was not as great as his looks. For me a boy has to be kind and nice as well as cute, and Peter has not exactly been Mr. Congeniality!"

"Maybe it's all an act and deep inside he's really shy," Chrissy suggested. Caroline spluttered with laughter.

"And maybe I'm really Brooke Shields in disguise," she said. "Go on, go and wiggle your bikini for him. Only for heaven sakes, don't do anything dangerous. You have to set an example for your campers!"

Chrissy turned back and smiled. "Don't worry," she said. "Nothing in the world would make me risk another attempt at mouth to mouth from Elizabeth!" Caroline watched her thoughtfully as she hurried into her cabin.

Chapter 10

The next morning Caroline woke to muffled giggles and scufflings. A wind blew in her face. For a moment she wondered what Chrissy was doing, opening windows so early in the morning and why she was giggling. Then she remembered that she wasn't at home in her own bedroom. She opened her eyes and sat up. The five other occupants of her bunk were crowded at the window, peering through the makeshift towel curtains, and whispering excitedly.

"What's so interesting?" Caroline asked, still half-asleep. They all spun around at the sound of her voice.

"Oh, nothing," they mumbled, as they instantly pretended to be busy brushing their hair and getting dressed.

At least they seem to be getting along well now,
she thought to herself. *Yesterday it seemed that
they had all taken an instant dislike to each other.
Maybe I've helped them to understand what
camp is about!*

"Breakfast in twenty minutes," she said pleasantly. "Everyone sleep well?"

"Are you kidding? I was freezing," Jodi complained.

"I would have been freezing too if I hadn't
brought my down sleeping bag," Kendall said,
"but I couldn't sleep anyway because someone
was snoring all night."

"It was Francesca," Sam said.

"It was not. I do not snore. Only mouth breath-
ers snore, and my orthodontist says that I am not
a mouth breather, so there," Francesca said
firmly.

"It must have been Rachel then," Kendall said,
frowning at her.

"It wasn't me, because I was awake all night,
watching the window in case a bear came in."

The others giggled at this.

"If anyone came in, it would be that cute boy
with the punk haircut, coming to see me," Jodi
said. "Someone told me his name is Greg. What a
great name. Greg. Greg and Jodi, Jodi and Greg."

Sam interrupted with loud gagging noises. Caroline sensed another fight developing and scrambled into her robe. "I'm going down to the
showers," she said. "You'd better move if you
want to get to breakfast on time."

"Those showers are cold!" Kendall said in horror. "I wonder if they make portable solar heaters? By the time I've finished my list of supplies that I need, my dad will have to hire an entire bus. This place isn't like the brochures pictured it."

She picked up a half-written letter from the table. "When my dad hears how miserable I am, he'll rush right up here—even if my mother doesn't want him to."

"Your parents are divorced too?" Sam asked.

"Yup," Kendall replied. "My mom didn't want me to spend the summer with my dad and his girlfriend, and besides, she wanted to go on a cruise to some island."

Caroline sensed a friendship brewing as she left Sam and Kendall talking and headed for the shower.

This would be a perfect camp for dieters, Caroline thought as she ate breakfast with her campers. She chewed her way through cornflakes, glad that she had not taken any of the scrambled eggs. The girls were camouflaging hard globs of scrambled eggs with oceans of ketchup.

"This stuff is totally uneatable," Kendall complained.

"Inedible," Francesca corrected.

"Whatever," Kendall snapped. "Luckily I had previous experience and came prepared." She reached into her large overall pocket and pulled out a packet of minidonuts.

"You brought your own food?" Rachel asked, impressed.

"Sure. I'm very fussy about what I eat," Kendall said. "I don't want to eat this slime."

"Me either!" Rachel wailed.

Suddenly her entire group pushed their plates away in what appeared to be a hunger strike.

"Let's have one of your donuts, Kendall," Jodi insisted, grabbing the packet of donuts.

"I only brought enough for me," Kendall said, cramming one into her mouth as she finished speaking.

"Oh, come on, don't hog them all," Jodi insisted. "Can't you share them? I'll trade you something for them."

"You should have come prepared like I did," Kendall said. "Sorry, Charlie."

"Boy, are you a meanie!" Jodi said. She tried to grab Kendall's arm and knocked over the bottle of ketchup. A wave of ketchup shot out onto Kendall's overalls. Kendall leaped up with a scream of horror.

"Look what you did!" she yelled.

"I didn't do it on purpose!" Jodi begged. "It was an accident."

"Oh my goodness, she's bleeding!" Rachel shrieked. "Look at all the blood!"

By now, all the other campers were jumping around, trying to see what the commotion was about.

"Sit down, everyone. It's only ketchup," Caroline said, trying to calm them. "Jodi, go with her to the bathroom and rinse it out in cold water before it stains."

"Stains! She's ruined my overalls."

"They're only old overalls, Kendall," Sam said. "They're all faded!"

"Only old overalls?" Kendall's voice rose to a shriek. "Do you know where these came from? They came from a boutique on Rodeo Drive. My father spent a fortune on them."

"In which case I'd say you were gypped," Sam said. "They look like early Thrift Shop to me!"

"I think you're all hateful," Kendall wailed. "I want to go home. I'm going to see the camp director and demand that he let me phone my daddy."

"Having fun?" Peter asked as he passed by Caroline. Caroline had to stop herself from aiming the ketchup bottle in his direction.

By the time breakfast was over and Caroline had soothed Kendall's hysterics, she was almost ready to fall asleep again. She watched as the campers divided up for their afternoon activities, grateful that she and Chrissy had volunteered to do arts 'n' crafts. It was a beautiful warm morning so most of the kids opted for a free swim or canoeing instruction. She sat, enjoying the warm sun, macraméing a key chain.

"If camp was always like this, I'd like it better," she commented to Chrissy. "There seems to be a crisis every minute with my girls."

"Mine are fine," Chrissy said. "Maybe it's the air of leadership that makes the difference."

"Oh, shut up," Caroline growled under her breath. "You're just lucky, that's all. Tell the kids in my group to follow you and they'd all go the other way. I'm not looking forward to the compass orientation hike. I'm going to have to keep them roped to me or Jodi will slip off after the boys and Kendall will have an off-road vehicle flown in for her to ride on."

Chrissy giggled. "We'll go together, OK? That way one of us can read the map and the other one can stop the kids from wandering off."

"Good idea," Caroline said. "By the way, what are you doing for your campfire skit tonight? We're going to work on ours during free time this afternoon, but I don't have any brilliant ideas."

"Me neither," Chrissy said. "I guess we really missed out, not being Girl Scouts. The ex-Scouts have millions of clever ideas. I bet Elizabeth will do something to show off!"

"The dance of the seven veils, perhaps?" Caroline asked. "For a special person's benefit?"

"That's not such a bad idea," Chrissy said pensively.

"Don't even think of it!" Caroline warned. "You would pull off the wrong veil and trip over it."

Chrissy laughed. "I don't think it's really me, but it would be nice to show off a little. Something I can do that nobody else can. I'll work on it, just in case!"

During the next few hours Caroline wondered more than once what Chrissy would come up with this time to impress Peter. She hardly dared to think of some of the things that might be passing through Chrissy's mind. *I hope she won't do anything too dumb,* she worried, *but when she's determined like this, it's impossible to stop her! I wish she'd see that Peter is not worth all this effort. He and Elizabeth really deserve each other—two snobs together.*

Meanwhile Caroline tried to concentrate on what her own campers could do for the evening skit. When she asked them for suggestions after lunch, they didn't seem to be exactly brimming over with enthusiasm.

"We could do the skit where we put our hands into shoes and kneel down and do a dwarves' dance," Sam suggested. "We did that at Girl Scout camp last year. It was a blast."

"Sounds rather juvenile to me," Jodi said to Kendall. "I'd rather mime to a Madonna tape."

"No outlets for the tape player, remember?" Sam reminded them.

"My tape player works on batteries also," Kendall informed the group.

"We could mime to one of my tapes," Jodi added.

"We could dance," Francesca chimed in.

Caroline's eyes lit up at the mere mention of dancing. *Now that's something I can do probably better than anyone else, including Elizabeth.* Finally, an idea interested both Caroline and the girls.

"I'll go get my tapes," Kendall said.

"Me too," Jodi added.

"How about Madonna?" Jodi asked.

"Janet Jackson?" Sam asked.

"How 'bout Cyndi Lauper?" Francesca asked. "We could all do a skit to 'Girls Just Wanna Have Fun.'"

"And I could choreograph it," Caroline added, just as excited about the idea as her campers were.

The girls were all busy deciding on a song and costumes, when suddenly the door of their cabin started to open mysteriously. All six of them turned to look, and seconds later the girls were all up on their beds and screaming as a fat skunk waddled in. Caroline looked at it in horror as it began to make its way down the center aisle, pausing to sniff at a bag on the floor.

"Keep calm, keep calm!" Caroline yelled, waving her hands dramatically. "You know what happens if you scare a skunk. Just keep quiet and maybe it will go out the way it came in. Just stay still up on your beds. Don't move or you'll scare it."

The noise level fell to gentle whimpering.

"Skunks usually have rabies," Francesca's dry voice said, cutting through Rachel's sobs. Don't let it bite you."

In a matter of seconds, all five girls were huddled on Caroline's bed. Once again, Caroline had to hide her own fears and anxieties.

"We're all going to be bitten to death. We're all going to die!" Rachel wailed, clinging to Caroline so determinedly that Caroline was unable to move. The skunk had now reached the far end of the cabin. Caroline stood up, with Rachel still clinging to her. "Quick, everybody out while we've got a chance. We'll get Mr. Ed to deal with it."

The girls needed no urging. They fought and pushed to get through the doorway first. Caroline came down the steps last with Rachel wrapped around her neck.

The first person she saw at the bottom of the steps was Peter. He was sitting on the steps of his cabin, watching her with his usual amused expression.

"What's the hurry this time?" he asked. "Another bear?"

"This time there's a skunk in my cabin," Caroline snapped, "and it is not a kitten and it is not a stuffed toy. It is a real, live, walking, skunk, and it could have rabies."

Peter stood up. "In here?" he asked. "A skunk?" He started to go up the steps.

"Be careful," Caroline called. "He could spray you."

He looked back with a small smile and appeared again a few seconds later with the skunk in his arms. Caroline and her girls froze in terror as he came toward them.

"Are you crazy?" Caroline called. "You're that anxious for a rabies shot?"

Peter shook his head slowly. "Nah, this is Wilbur. He's been de-scented."

"Wilbur?"

"Yeah, you know little Ozzie in my bunk? It's his pet skunk. He brought him along, and I didn't have the heart to confiscate him."

Thoughts were beginning to take shape in Caroline's head. Fear was being overwhelmed by anger. She remembered the door slowly opening, the skunk suddenly appearing, terrifying her girls.

"You did this, didn't you?" she yelled. "You and your crummy little boys played a trick on us. I bet it gave you a good laugh to hear the poor terrified girls screaming. Well, I think that's pretty low. It does fit, though—a skunk as your mascot! It matches your personality."

She looked from Peter to the grinning faces of the little boys who had now appeared around the side of their cabin.

"Why don't you ask your little angels what they were doing this morning," Peter asked sweetly.

"What are you talking about?" Caroline demanded.

Peter looked hard at Caroline. "You mean you don't know? You didn't help them?"

"I'm sure whatever it was, it was pretty harmless compared to a skunk," Caroline said.

"Oh, yeah?" Peter asked. "Harmless, eh, girls? You should have seen our cabin right after breakfast."

"What were they doing?" Caroline asked. She turned to face her campers, who were all suddenly rather red-faced and embarrassed.

"Let me tell you," Peter said, stepping toward

Caroline. "Your sweet little angels visited the lake this morning, and not to swim. They collected ants and put them in our cabin. When we came back from breakfast, the place was crawling with them. I don't think that's very harmless, do you?"

Caroline felt her cheeks glowing bright crimson. She wanted to laugh, but kept a stern face. "No," she said, turning to her girls. "I think that's just terrible."

The girls all wriggled uncomfortably under her stare.

"It was only fun," Jodi said at last.

"We just paid them back because they squirted us with water down at the lake yesterday. They had squirt guns. We got soaked," Kendall said with a pout.

"At least water is harmless," Caroline said. "Ants in your food and clothing are not."

The girls giggled. Caroline frowned. "Go back in the cabin and wait for me," she said. "Because of this, I think you guys ought to miss the campfire tonight."

The girls trooped into the cabin, one by one. Caroline watched them, secretly amazed at her power. At least they had obeyed her. At least that was one step in the right direction.

Peter turned to his boys. "And you boys back, too," he said. "I know the ants were a mean trick, but so was the skunk." The boys grinned at one another and shuffled up the steps. Peter and Caroline stood facing each other.

"Look," he said at last. "I'm sorry about the

skunk. I had no idea they were going to pull that trick."

"I'm sorry about the ants too," Caroline said. "That must have been a real mess."

"You'd better believe it," Peter agreed. "One of the boys had a box of cookies. It was covered with ants. Disgusting."

"I'll try and keep them in line in the future," Caroline said. "It's not easy."

Peter grinned. "I know," he said. "Especially your kids. Are all girls of eleven such precocious little brats?"

"I wasn't," Caroline said.

"I think I'll get a second opinion on that from your cousin," Peter said smoothly.

"That won't do you any good. She didn't even know me when I was eleven."

"Oh, why not?"

"Because she was still living back in . . ." Caroline stopped herself abruptly. The trouble with one lie, she thought, was that it led to a whole pack of other lies. "Because our two families were not getting along in those days," she said. She looked away, angry at herself. "I'd better go see what those little monsters are up to."

Five repentant faces looked up at her as she came in.

"We're sorry, Caroline," Kendall said.

"It was only a joke," Jodi added.

"We won't do it again," Sam chimed in.

"I just want you to know that I was not in

agreement with it in the first place," Francesca said coldly.

"Yes, you were. You caught the biggest ants!" Rachel accused.

"Only to show solidarity," Francesca said.

"Cut it out, you guys," Sam yelled. "What we wanted to say, Caroline, is that we're sorry we let you down and made you look like a fool in front of that guy."

"Especially because he's so cute and you obviously like him," Jodi chimed in.

Caroline's mouth opened. "Who said anything about me liking him?" she demanded.

"That was obvious," Kendall said smoothly. "You blushed as soon as he looked at you. And he does have a gorgeous body!"

"Well, for your information, I am not wild about him," Caroline said. "Every time we meet, he manages to score all the points, and I don't think that is the basis for a future friendship. In addition to which, I think his attention has already been captured. So don't go getting any ideas."

"We won't, Caroline," Jodi said. "Now let's get on with our skit. We want it to be good tonight."

Chapter 11

Caroline did not have a chance to talk to Chrissy before the campfire. Chrissy and her girls had disappeared into the woods to practice in secret. Caroline just hoped it was not the dance of the seven veils that they were practicing! Her own girls threw themselves with enthusiasm in their skit. They knew the words to the song they had finally settled on by heart, and Caroline even taught them a simple dance routine. She liked the skit even more when the girls insisted that she participate in it with them.

The skit went well at the campfire, and the other counselors complimented Caroline on a job well done. Then it was Chrissy's turn. Mr. Ed looked down at his program and announced, "Presenting—Chrissy's Cowgirls!"

With that Chrissy and her kids galloped into the circle on imaginary horses, whooping and shouting like old ranchhands. Somehow, Chrissy had managed to find Western hats for everyone, although some of the girls struggled to keep them on their heads.

First, the campers performed a complete Western horse routine, crisscrossing and jumping fences they had made. Then Chrissy appeared in the middle, swinging a rope around her head.

Mama mia! Caroline thought. *She really is going to do her lassoing demonstration. I hope she really does know how to do it!*

"And now Cowgirl Chrissy will show us how to really lasso!" one of the girls announced.

Chrissy whirled the rope around her head until it whistled and then dropped it neatly over a stick on the other side of the circle. Everyone clapped. One of her girls stood very straight and still and Chrissy dropped the lasso neatly over her. More applause. Chrissy's face was flushed with success.

"Back in the Old West," a small, blushing camper announced, "the cowboy and the cowgirl had to be always alert, quick on the draw, able to get their man with a gun . . . or with a lasso!" As the announcer darted back to her seat, Chrissy spun the lasso out into the audience. She had obviously intended to lasso Peter, but as she was throwing, Elizabeth leaned close to Peter and put her arms around him, so that the lasso fell neatly over their two heads, drawing them very close together. The campers cheered and whistled.

Peter looked uncomfortable, but Elizabeth calmly took the lasso off. "Thanks for the help, but we don't need anything to bring us closer together!" she said to Chrissy as she handed her back the rope.

Caroline was glad she was in the darkness, beyond the light of the fire, because she didn't want Chrissy to see her grinning. As hard as she tried, she couldn't stop herself. *Poor old Chrissy!* she thought. *Everything she tries to do with Peter goes wrong. Maybe she should admit defeat and start getting interested in somebody else.*

The campfire drew to a close with songs and toasted s'mores, a graham cracker sandwich stuffed with chocolate and a toasted marshmallow, which Caroline was quickly learning to love. As Caroline shepherded her girls to their bunkhouse Chrissy caught up with her.

"Am I doomed to failure, or what?" she demanded. "Do you think some bad fairy put a spell on me?"

"Who's the bad fairy? Elizabeth?" Caroline asked.

"I wouldn't be surprised," Chrissy growled. "She always fouls up all my schemes!"

"Maybe it's because you're scheming, Chrissy," Caroline said gently. "Schemes don't often go the way you plan them. Often they ricochet back on you. Sometimes you just have to sit back and let life happen."

"You mean sit back and watch Elizabeth get my guy!" Chrissy said.

"If she's scheming, she won't get him either," Caroline soothed. "The guy is not stupid. He's not going to fall for any girl because she lassos him or even grabs him."

"Oh, no?" Chrissy asked. "Maybe he's more stupid than you think!"

Caroline followed Chrissy's gaze across the deserted campground. Under the shadow of a large tree two figures were standing together. Stretching to get a better view, they saw the silhouette of a boy and a girl. As they watched, Elizabeth slid her arms around the boy's neck. The girls turned away as the couple began to kiss.

"I really think you'd better admit defeat now, Chrissy," Caroline said, taking her arm as she led her back to the cabin. "It looks like Elizabeth has definitely won this contest!"

In the middle of the night Caroline awoke to a terrifying sound. Someone close to her was screaming and moaning.

"Let go of me! Leave me alone! You're hurting me!"

Caroline sat up in bed, her heart pounding, her eyes peering through the darkness to see what was happening. With a trembling hand she switched on the lamp beside the bed. The single bulb cast just enough light for her to see that there weren't any strange figures in the room and that nobody was being attacked. All five girls were in their beds.

"A nightmare," Caroline told herself, her heart still hammering so loudly that she found it hard to breathe. "One of the girls had a nightmare, that's all. I bet it's Rachel. Poor little Rachel, I bet she's always having nightmares."

Caroline swung her feet onto the cool wooden floor, then tiptoed over to Rachel's bed, but she found Rachel sleeping peacefully, looking really angelic as the light fell on her little round cheeks.

"Don't you see you're hurting me!" the moaning went on. "Just let go of me, please!"

Caroline turned to see the bed in the corner bouncing as somebody tossed and turned. It wasn't Rachel at all who was having the nightmare; it was Kendall! Caroline sat on Kendall's bed and stroked her hair. "It's OK," she whispered. "You're only dreaming."

Kendall thrashed even more to shake herself free of Caroline's hand.

"Leave me alone. Let go of me!" she screamed. Her pretty face was bathed in sweat. Caroline picked her up by the shoulders. "Kendall," she said firmly. "Wake up! You're having a bad dream. Wake up!"

A sudden draft behind Caroline made her spin around. Peter stood in the doorway, his shadowy form as perfect as ever in a knee-length terrycloth robe.

"What's going on in here?" he asked in between yawns.

Kendall moaned loudly.

"It's Kendall. She's having a nightmare," Caroline said, growing hot under Peter's suspicious gaze.

"Do you need any help?" he asked.

"No, thank you," Caroline answered shortly. She had the situation under control. At least she wanted Peter to think she did. She turned back to him. He was still standing by the door.

"I can handle it," she said firmly. "Just go."

"Oh, OK then," he said hesitantly. Kendall was moaning incoherently. He paused at the door.

"I'm fine. . . really," Caroline snapped.

"OK, if you're sure."

"I'm sure." *He probably thinks I'm responsible for her nightmare*, Caroline thought angrily. That wasn't the only reason why she was angry. The picture of Peter and Elizabeth kissing still lingered in her mind.

He closed the door quietly behind him. That small sound made Kendall suddenly open her eyes. She looked around in panic, gradually focusing on Caroline. "What happened?" she asked.

"You just had a terrible nightmare, nearly scared me to death," Caroline said. "I couldn't wake you."

Kendall nodded. "I get them sometimes."

"Are you OK now?"

"I need a drink of water."

"I'll come with you," Caroline said. She helped her up and holding her hand led her like a little child down the steps and over to the drinking fountain.

"It's nice out here," Kendall said on the way back. "I think I'd like to sit on the steps for a while. I'm still feeling pretty shaky."

"Me too," Caroline said.

"I guess I yell pretty loud, huh?" Kendall asked.

"Very loud. You even woke Peter in the next cabin."

"I'm sorry."

"You couldn't help it. Are you OK?" Caroline asked gently. "You looked terrified. Do you know what those nightmares are about?"

"Oh, I know all right," Kendall said quietly. "They're always the same. They're about my mother and father."

"Your mother and father?" Caroline was surprised.

"They each have hold of one of my arms, and they are pulling me in half. They don't seem to realize that they are hurting me. They just keep on pulling and pulling," Kendall said. She looked up at Caroline. "I understand the dream. They've been fighting over me ever since the divorce. Sometimes I feel like I'm being pulled in half. If I talk to my dad, my mom gets mad at me, and if I talk to my mom, my dad is jealous. I feel like I have to watch everything I say and do so that I don't upset them both." She looked down at her hands again. "That's why I'm here, of course. It made it easy. This way they didn't have to fight about who got me and for how long. My mother was going away, and I really didn't want to stay with my dad."

"I thought you loved your father. You've been threatening to phone him nonstop," Caroline commented.

"He pays for things," Kendall said simply. "Nothing's too much money for him. He gives me everything I ask for, except time, I guess. He doesn't have any of that to spare."

"And your mom?" Caroline asked. "Does she have more time for you?"

Kendall laughed. "Are you kidding? I have to make an appointment to say good morning between her facial and her aerobics class. She's very dedicated to staying young and beautiful."

Caroline looked at the young girl as if she was seeing her for the first time. She thought of her own family and how lucky she was: Everybody sharing news around the table; her mother cancelling appointments when she was sick; her father sitting on her bed reading to her when she got the chicken pox at Kendall's age.

"I'm sorry, Kendall," she said. "I bet they really both love you, but they don't know how to show it. Why don't you write them both a letter while you are up here. Let them know how you feel. Maybe it will change things."

"Maybe," Kendall said. She got up stiffly. "I'm keeping you awake," she said. "Sorry about that." She glanced into the cabin. "You . . . won't say anything about this to the others?"

"Of course not," Caroline said. "And any time you want to talk . . . That's what counselors are for."

Kendall smiled, a soft, little-girl smile for the first time. "Thanks," she said.

Caroline sat alone on the steps after Kendall had gone back to bed. She felt very grown up suddenly, and cringed at the thought of being responsible for five not-so-little girls. What a responsibility it was. Each one came with her own set of problems and dreams. It wasn't just up to Caroline to keep them in line and make sure they got home safely, it was up to her to understand, to be their friend.

Chapter 12

The next morning Caroline awoke, feeling very groggy, to the sound of raised voices. She instantly recognized one of the voices as Kendall's.

"You did it on purpose," Kendall was saying.

"I did not. It was an accident, I swear!" Jodi exclaimed in a high-pitched whine.

Caroline rolled over to face them. "What's the problem now?" she asked.

"She knocked the towel down from the window, just when I was changing," Kendall said, scowling at Jodi. "She did it on purpose because that boy Scott in the next cabin likes me better than her."

"I did not do it on purpose. I just walked past and it fell down," Jodi whined. "Besides, you're wrong about Scott. He likes me!"

Caroline couldn't help smiling to herself as she lay back on her pillow, gazing up at the naked light bulb. Once again, things were back to normal.

The noise erupted again. She climbed from her bed. "Put the towel back in place by the time I get back from the bathroom, Jodi," she commanded. Then she slipped on her robe and made her way across to the bathrooms.

On her way she encountered a strange figure. It was swathed in towels from head to foot and looked like a Bedouin lost from a camel caravan. As she approached it, a muffled sound came from beneath the towels. "Hi, Cara!"

"Chrissy? What on earth are you doing? Playing mummy?"

"Not exactly. I didn't want anyone to see me," Chrissy said in a muffled voice.

"Why not?"

"Come back into the bathroom. I'll show you," Chrissy said, turning back into the doorway. Caroline followed, mystified and amused. Chrissy always had to dramatize situations!

Safely inside Chrissy lowered the towel from her face. "Because of this," she said.

Caroline gasped in horror. "Chrissy! What is it? You're bright red and puffy!"

"I was hoping you'd tell me," Chrissy said. "Do you think it's the measles or something?"

"How do you feel?"

"Itchy," Chrissy said. "Itchy all over."

She held out an arm for Caroline to examine. It

too was covered in angry red blotches, some of them blistered. Suddenly Caroline guessed what was wrong.

"I know what it is—you've got poison oak!" she exclaimed.

"This is terrible, Cara. I feel like the human radish," Chrissy wailed. "When will it go away?"

"It usually takes a few days, I think," Caroline said. "And you must make sure you don't touch other people or their clothing. It's very contagious."

"This is more than terrible," Chrissy sighed, "I'll be a social outcast. They'll lock me in a cage and everyone will laugh at me! This whole camp was a big mistake, Cara. Everything's gone wrong for me from the start. Now Peter will never get a chance to know me better. He'll run and hide when he sees me coming, or, worse still, he'll laugh. I should never have come here. I'm being punished for not going straight home to my family."

"Oh, Chrissy," Caroline said, reaching out to touch her cousin and then quickly changing her mind. "I'm so sorry, but it's not the end of the world. It will be over in a few days and I know everyone will be sympathetic. Come on, I'll take you to see the nurse and see what she recommends."

"I hope she recommends some anti-itch medicine," Chrissy said, wriggling around inside her towels. "This is already driving me crazy. Someone will have to take over my kids for me, and I won't be able to go on the hike with you."

"Never mind, it can't be helped," Caroline said,
trying to hide the sinking feeling she felt at
having to face the hike alone. She had never had
any experience with maps and compasses, and
she did not feel at all competent for such a
mission. She wasn't even sure that she could
recognize poison oak or poison anything else!
Still, poor Chrissy is much worse off than me, she
thought as she crossed the compound with her
cousin. *I'll survive the hunt OK, but she's got
several days of itching ahead of her!*

She left Chrissy comfortably settled in the
infirmary with a pitcher of ice water beside her
and some old magazines scrounged from other
counselors to read.

"The good life," she joked to Chrissy. "Better
than struggling over hillsides, following a map
and falling down ravines, I'd say."

"At least you're not itching," Chrissy growled,
unable to joke. "I don't know whether to drink
that ice water or splash it all over me."

Elizabeth came to speak to Caroline that morning. "Your poor cousin," she said. "What a mess!
I've never seen anyone swell up quite so much
with poison oak. I went in to try and cheer her
up, but I guess she was feeling too miserable to
appreciate it."

Caroline thought privately that seeing Elizabeth would be the last thing in the world that
might cheer Chrissy up. Apart from having Jeff
shipped in, or placing a magical spell on Peter,

she couldn't think of anything that would uplift her spirits right now.

She's right, Caroline thought. *She has had one disaster after another for the past couple of weeks! First Jeff going away, then being rescued by Elizabeth, then the lassoing, and now the poison oak. Things can't get much worse for her. It can only get better from here on.*

She went to round up her campers for the prehike meeting. Mr. Ed handed out maps and compasses to each of the counselors and explained that this event was a competition. Every group would be passing checkpoints in a different order so that no one could just follow another group. The campers who managed to pass each of the checkpoints and collect their items first would win points toward the intercabin competition. He refreshed their memory on how to use a compass and map and wished them luck. Caroline felt that she needed the luck very badly. All the other counselors had previous experience and knew exactly what Mr. Ed was talking about. The other counselors were excited and ready to begin. Even their campers looked fit and ready to go, in contrast to her own, who looked as if they might collapse or mutiny after the first slope. Caroline glanced up and saw Horrible Howard, the little creep from Berkeley, staring at her again. He always seemed to be staring at her. If she ever made the mistake of smiling or even acknowledging him, he would scurry across to spout computer terminology at her. *Maybe I*

should get him to team up with me! she thought
with a grin. With the least encouragement she
could make him do all her map reading for her—
but there would be consequences. On second
thought, she decided, she'd rather risk getting
lost.

"This should take about four hours," Mr. Ed
called as everyone got ready. "I hope you all ate
a hearty snack because you won't get supper
until you get back. And remember, above all,
stick together and be careful!"

"Will it be dangerous?" Rachel whispered, slipping her hand into Caroline's.

"It will be fine," Caroline said, giving her hand
a squeeze. "Just a long walk, like a treasure hunt.
We can go slow if you want."

"OK." Rachel skipped along happily beside her.

Caroline clutched the map and compass in her
hand as she rounded up her campers. They were
hardly more enthusiastic about the hunt than she
was.

"Do we have to go?" Kendall asked. "My foot
hurts. I twisted it getting out of a canoe."

"I'm tired," Jodi moaned. "I don't want to hike
up a mountain."

"What if we get lost?" Rachel asked suddenly.
"Who will find us?"

"Come on, you babies," Sam interrupted. "This
is what you came to camp for, isn't it? It can be
fun. Don't be such blockheads."

"You're a big pill," Kendall muttered.

"There's no use arguing about it," Caroline said

firmly. "We all have to go on the hunt. It is a required activity and I'm going to need everyone's help to find the checkpoints, so let's get going."

They marched off in silence, down past the lake. Other teams headed up the hills, scattering until all sounds of voices had died away. The only sounds left were the soft swish of their feet over pine needles and the gentle sigh of the wind in the high branches. Caroline consulted her map.

"Here, Francesca, you're good at this sort of thing," she said. "We have to go northeast for a quarter of a mile."

Francesca peered at the map. "That's up that hill over there. We should've counted paces when we left the camp, then we'd know exactly how far we had to go."

They tramped up the slope and found a plastic bag marked by a blue ribbon attached to a big old cedar tree at the top.

"The first checkpoint!" Francesca exclaimed in her first sign of enthusiasm since she arrived. She grabbed the bag and took out a piece of paper."

"Let us look," Caroline said. "Let me see that."

Francesca held out the paper and they all peered at it. "It says east fifty yards to the big split rock and then north another quarter of a mile," Francesca read aloud. "That sounds easy enough. Come on, let's go."

"What's the hurry? My foot hurts," Kendall complained.

"We might win," Francesca said.

"Big deal."

"Whoever wins the whole contest gets an ice cream party," Rachel reminded her. "I'd like to win. Come on, let's hurry."

They started down the next slope. "Wait a minute, are we going east?" Caroline asked, checking her map.

"The sun sets in the west, doesn't it?" Francesca asked. "And it's right on our back now."

The trees became thicker as they descended lower and lower. They had to push their way through dead branches.

"I'm sure we've gone fifty yards by now," Caroline said, glancing around worriedly. "Let me look at that map again."

"There's a stream down there," Sam suggested. "See where that is."

Caroline consulted the map. There didn't appear to be any stream where she thought they were heading. She didn't say anything to the others, but she searched until she found a faint blue line crossing the map. "This must be it, Sugar Creek," she said, trying to sound confident. "I think we must have passed the rock we were looking for. The trees were so thick, we might just have missed it. Maybe we should start heading north like the instructions said. The checkpoint will be in a pretty obvious place."

They crossed the stream by walking on large rocks. The water looked cool and inviting, murmuring as it danced over pebbles and splashed down miniature waterfalls. All the girls wanted to stop and play.

"Oh, come on, Caroline. We really don't care about winning, and I do need to soak my feet," Kendall said.

Nobody disagreed.

"Well, just for a few minutes then," Caroline said doubtfully. Soon there were squeals of laughter from all of the girls as they danced in and out of the icy water. Caroline watched them. *They are all little kids underneath,* she thought. *They just pretend to be bored and sophisticated. Maybe they will learn to loosen up in camp.*

She was jarred from her thoughts by Rachel's screams. "Caroline, what's that on your shoulder? It's huge!"

Caroline whirled around, brushing furiously as she caught something moving out of the corner of her eye. The others clustered around.

"It was only a big old dragonfly," Sam said with amusement. "You weren't scared of that, were you, Caroline?"

The dragonfly took off again, zooming around Caroline's head. She could hear the whirring noise of its wings. Its body looked very large.

She remembered that it wasn't a good idea to let your campers know you were afraid of something—especially bugs. "Oh, no," she managed to say. "I'm not scared of a dragonfly. I just couldn't see what it was, that's all."

"But won't it sting us to death?" Rachel asked, cowering each time it zoomed over.

"Dragonflies are harmless, dodo," Sam said, attempting to catch it as it flew past.

The other girls were obviously not convinced that dragonflies were harmless. Without a word from Caroline they all began to pull on their shoes again.

"We'd better be going," Kendall said. "We've wasted too much time here. We'll never win that ice cream if we don't hurry."

"Yeah," Jodi agreed. "We don't want those creepy boys in the next cabin to beat us."

They crossed the stream and began to make their way across the rocky slope ahead. This time the path was tough to cross because there were uneven boulders between the trees, and the girls had to jump and avoid low branches. The slope got steeper and steeper until suddenly the trees ended. Directly in front was a bald mountaintop with a view of snowcapped peaks in the distance.

"The checkpoint must be somewhere up here," Caroline said hopefully. It looked like a logical spot for a checkpoint. "Let's climb on up to the summit."

The others followed her, muttering. As they rounded the big rock that formed the summit, the first thing they saw were a pair of legs and feet, sticking out. Rachel screamed. The legs and feet disappeared.

"Well, look who is it? It's that Kendall and Jodi!" a little boy's voice squeaked. The girls had come face to face with Peter's group. Caroline felt an enormous sigh of relief run through her body.

She was safe. She could get the girls home again.

"What are you doing up here?" Peter asked. He was propped in the shade of the big rock. "Two groups aren't supposed to cross paths. Did you miss a checkpoint?"

Caroline was just about to admit that she was totally lost but quickly closed her mouth. Why did this creep always have to see her in an inferior position? Every time they met he had another opportunity to score points. She could imagine him gloating as he said, "Lost already? You've only been out an hour or so!"

"We just climbed up here to get the view," Caroline said. Her girls had already flopped down into the shade beside Peter's boys and were busy exchanging information.

"So did we," Peter said. "Pretty good, isn't it?"

"We've already found three checkpoints," she heard a squeaky little boy's voice boast. "How many have you found?"

"Do you want a drink?" Peter asked, bringing out a canteen. "You all look pretty hot."

Caroline refused, but all the girls accepted. They settled themselves comfortably in the shade.

"I suppose we'd better be going again," Peter said as he recapped his flask. "You, too, if you want to make it back before dark. Are you sure you don't need some help? We could head back down this hill together to our next checkpoint and you could take it from there."

"No, that's all right, thank you," Caroline said

stiffly. "I'm sure we'll do just fine. We'll just rest a minute and then we'll be on our way."

She lay back into the cool shade, feasting her eyes on the glittering snow peaks in the distance and the shimmering blue hills folded beneath them. She wasn't at all sure that she wanted to move, ever.

She was roused by Peter's voice, soft but firm. "Don't anybody move. There's a rattlesnake down by that rock."

Caroline looked at the small brownish snake, then at Peter. *Oh sure*, she thought. *Another little joke! We'll all panic and run away screaming, and then they'll tell us it was only a gopher snake or something.*

She got up slowly. "Don't worry, we can handle rattlesnakes," she said. As she spoke she picked up a dead pine branch from the rock. She walked across to the snake. *It's not even rattling,* she thought. *There is no way this is a rattlesnake. I'll show him once and for all!* She slid the stick under the snake and then gently flicked it so that the snake went slithering down the hill and into the trees.

Everyone started to cheer. "Wow, did you see that? She touched a snake! Hey, that was cool."

"Hey, I'm impressed," Peter said, looking hard at her. He got to his feet. "You're sure you don't want to come with us?"

"Quite sure."

"OK. Well, you can obviously take care of yourselves. . . ." He hesitated on the rim of the hill. "Well . . . we'll see you back at camp then, I guess."

"I guess we will."

"Well, good luck."

"Good luck to you too!"

Caroline stood motionless as the group slowly disappeared into the trees.

Chapter 13

The sound of feet moving through the under-brush died away, and was replaced by the melancholy sigh of the wind through the rocks. Caroline moved to the edge of the plateau.

"We'd better be going down too," she said. The sun, she noticed, was no longer comfortably high in the sky. It was rapidly plunging toward the blue line of western hills. The thought crossed her mind that if they followed Peter's trail quickly enough, he could lead them back to safety and never know it.

"Oh, do we have to?" Jodi whined. "I have the biggest blister."

"Let me see." Caroline eased off her sneaker. "Wow, that is pretty big, Jodi. I told you to wear socks!"

"My sneakers hurt when I wear socks," Jodi said, giving the blister a worried poke.

"Here." Caroline removed a tissue from her pocket and wrapped it around the toe. "This should take away some of the pressure and stop the rubbing."

"Thanks," Jodi said, standing up experimentally. "I feel much better."

"I'm tired," Rachel said quietly. "My legs don't want to go any more."

Caroline took her hand and pulled her up. "You don't want to have to spend the night out here, do you? You'd rather be safe in your own bed."

Rachel considered this. "I guess my legs will make it," she said.

Caroline led them down the hill, following Peter's group into the woods.

"Do you really know where we are?" Sam asked.

"Not exactly," Caroline lied.

"So why didn't we stick with Peter's group?" Kendall demanded.

"Because he's always right," Caroline said with a grin. "I didn't want him to think that we didn't know what we were doing."

"So how are we going to get back to the next checkpoint?" Francesca asked coldly. "We have no idea where we are on the map. There are a dozen hills like the one we've been on. We could be heading totally in the wrong direction."

"Are we going to be lost?" Rachel wailed.

"First," Caroline said, trying to sound completely calm and confident, "we are heading into the setting sun, which is west, and that's the right way. Second, we are following Peter's group; see where they've kicked up the pine needles? Only we won't let them know that we're following them, so we're going to keep very quiet."

"OK." The girls grinned to each other, liking this new adventure. Tracking the boys made them feel like spies. They made it down the mountain, stopping a couple of times to adjust Jodi's makeshift bandage, to get a bug out of Rachel's eye, and once to clean up a scratch on Sam's arm. Caroline tried to hurry them without letting them know how worried she really was. The sun, a red, glowing ball of fire, now barely hung over the horizon. Peter's group was moving at a far greater pace because the trail was increasingly hard to follow.

"I'm so tired," Rachel sighed. "We must have walked a million miles." She sank to the ground. The others followed her. Caroline started to urge them on, but decided to let them rest for a few minutes.

"I think I recognize this part," Sam said hopefully as they began again. "This is the rocky place where Kendall twisted her ankle."

They had left the sandy soil of the forest and now came to an area where pine trees grew at crazy angles—twisted and tormented—from the rocks. It did look similar to an area that they had covered earlier, which was encouraging. The bad part was that Peter's group had left no trail. The girls, much wearier than before, stumbled and slithered over the rocks. Their tempers flared and they grew more tired with every step. Caroline peered to the left and right, looking for just one clue to point them in the right direction.

"Doesn't that big tree up there look like the first checkpoint?" she asked hopefully.

The girls squinted at it, shielding their eyes from the last rays of the sun. "Maybe," Francesca agreed.

"You want me to run up and look?" Sam asked, glancing around at the rest of the group. The others sank down gratefully while Sam bounded up the hillside, only to return more slowly. "It wasn't," she said.

At that moment the sun sank behind the hill. Instantly, the air felt colder, and Caroline wished that she had insisted on the girls bringing jackets along.

"Which way do we go now?" Jodi asked in a quivering voice.

"Up here I guess," Caroline answered wearily. Her own forced confidence and cheerfulness were becoming very fragile. She felt that she might burst into tears at any moment. They slithered and climbed up the next slope, much steeper than the ones before. Caroline was hoping desperately that the hill would be high enough to give them a view of the lake or the smoke from the campfire. They reached the top, panting. Kendall screamed. Caroline grabbed at Sam who was about to take another step. The hill ended in a sheer drop, down into a ravine. Down below they could hear water churning. Only one sapling grew crazily from the wall. One more step and they would be lying among those jagged rocks. Caroline felt physically sick. If Sam had run ahead, as she often did . . . if Rachel had panicked . . . Up until now she had just talked a lot about being responsible for her campers, now it was staring her right in her face that their lives were literally in her hands. A chill ran up her spine.

"Let's go back down the way we came," she said, scanning the horizon and seeing only blue nothingness. "I don't want to risk losing anybody over the edge!" She took Rachel and Sam's hands. "All stay close together," she added.

By the time they were back at the bottom of the hill, the light was reduced to a gray twilight. Trees and rocks lost their color and took on menacing monster shapes.

"What's that?" Rachel whimpered. "There's a big animal up there watching us."

"It's only a big old dead tree," Caroline said reassuringly.

"I'm scared," Rachel said softly. "I don't want to go on any more. We don't know what horrible animals are up ahead."

"Most wild animals run away and hide if they hear you coming," Sam said.

That's good to know, Caroline thought. *But I should have known it before I came out here.* As her mind drifted over several possibilities, she remembered vaguely that one of the rules of the Outdoor Code was to stay put when you got lost and let a search party find you. They should have stopped as soon as she realized they were lost, not wandered into unexplored valleys. Caroline began to weigh decisions in her mind. It was already dark, and their chances of getting to safety were very small. Their chances of falling into a ravine, however, were pretty big. It really made sense to find somewhere safe to spend the night. *That bald hilltop would have been perfect,* she thought. *At least a helicopter would find us there if it came looking!* Caroline shivered as a chilly breeze rustled the brush nearby. *We must find a place to spend the night, out of the open air,* she decided.

She led them to a group of rocks, still sun-warmed, with overhangs that kept off the wind.

"We'll spend the night here," Caroline said.

"Aren't we going to try and get back?" Kendall asked.

"Not in the dark. We won't find the way."

"We could navigate by the stars," Francesca said. "You just get a fix on the North Star and . . ."

"No, thanks, Francesca," Caroline interrupted. "It's safer to stay here. Don't be scared. We are quite safe. We will be found early in the morning."

"No, we won't," Rachel sobbed. "Nobody will ever find us, and we'll be lost forever and all they'll find is our bones!"

"Nonsense," Caroline said, slipping an arm

around her shoulder. "They'll have search parties out first thing tomorrow morning. I bet we'll be back in time for breakfast."

"Logically speaking, I'd say our chances of being found are pretty slim," Francesca said. "I mean, the number of identical valleys—"

"Oh, shut up," Sam interrupted. "We don't need the voice of doom! Why don't we light a fire?"

"Great idea! A fire!" the others chimed in.

"I guess it's time to get out the emergency kit," Caroline said. She removed a book of matches from the small plastic bag in her pocket and helped the girls look for kindling.

"What good is a dinky fire when we don't have any food?" Kendall whined.

"We'll probably starve to death!" Rachel wailed.

Caroline had to laugh. "No, we won't, Rachel."

"We'll be fine, I promise." She looked from one face to the next, all very wide-eyed now, gazing at her with hope, as if she were their only link to safety.

"I'm sorry, guys," Caroline said quietly. "It's my fault I got you all lost. I guess I'm not much of a counselor . . ." her voice trailed off into silence. The wind whistled through the cracks in the rock.

"Yes, you are. You're OK as a counselor," Sam said.

"Counselors are supposed to be able to read maps and use compasses," Caroline said with a bitter laugh. "I'm not much good in the out-doors."

"But you're nice," Rachel said softly, "and you don't yell."

"And you take the time to help us," Jodi said. "You bandaged up my blister, and you got the fly out of Rachel's eye. I think you're OK."

"I think you're OK too," Kendall said. "You try real hard."

Somehow this was not very comforting to Caroline. She lay back against the rock, thinking the worst. She hadn't considered that she would probably get into big trouble when she got them back. Would parents sue her for putting their kids in such a dangerous situation? Would she lose her job?

I thought summer camp would be such a fun experience, she thought. *I thought it would be songs and games with little kids. Instead it's turned into one big nightmare. Talk about failure! I wish I was back at home right now with my parents to take care of me! I wish I wasn't responsible for these kids. I don't think I can take care of myself. I'm not ready for this!*

"Listen, what's that noise?" Rachel asked, sitting upright.

"Just my stomach growling," Sam said. "I'm hungry."

"No, not that noise—*that* noise!" Rachel exclaimed. "Can't you hear voices?"

Everyone was silent.

"I can hear them too," Kendall said, jumping

up. "It's the search party. They found us!"

"Yeah, we're saved!" Jodi said jumping up and down. "They're up there. Just above us. Let's go find them!"

"No need," Caroline said. "Stay put. They are coming this way."

"Over here!" the girls yelled.

There were answering cries, and soon boots began tramping down the rocks toward them.

"Oh, no!" a voice wailed as the first person slid down. "It's not camp at all! It's those girls again!"

Other figures began clambering down the rocks. Expressions and grunts of disappointment mixed with giggles and grins. Peter clambered down last of all. He stood facing Caroline.

"Did they send you out to find us?" he asked cautiously.

"Why, were you lost?" Caroline asked, equally cautious.

"Sort of."

"So you don't know the way back to camp either?" she asked with a sigh."

"Don't tell me you're lost too?" he asked.

"You guys really are lost?" Caroline asked, delight and despair mingling as she faced him.

"We've been lost for hours," he admitted.

"Us, too."

"You mean you were already lost when we met you up on the hill?"

"Right."

"So were we," Peter said with a short laugh. "I had hoped you would come with us so that together we could make it back, but you seemed so confident that I didn't want to admit to you that we were lost."

"I thought you seemed so confident," Caroline said in amazement. "I was sure you'd laugh at me again if I said we were lost."

"What do you mean, laugh at you again?"

"Because you're always laughing at me. Every time anything goes wrong, there you are grinning like a big ape."

"I am not!"

"What about that time with the bear?"

"Well, you have to admit that was funny."

"To you maybe. I really thought I came face to face with a bear in the girl's bathroom! And what about the poison oak . . . and Kendall's nightmare too? You always act so superior."

"Me, act superior?" Peter sounded astonished. "I heard this horrible screaming in the middle of the night. I came over to see what it was and you bit my head off as soon as you saw me. I'd say you were the one who was always acting superior."

"Me? I don't believe it."

"Come on, you acted like a snob," Peter said, his eyes challenging hers. "At school we're always teasing and putting each other down. I suppose everyone's so serious at Berkeley. I bet nobody makes jokes there."

Caroline wriggled her toes uncomfortably inside her sneakers. She wanted to open her mouth and blurt out that she didn't go there or to any other college, and that she was a little high school girl who, right now, was lost and frightened. But the kids were all crowded around them, waiting for them to make a decision.

"Will you two stop fighting and get us home safely?" one of the boys interrupted. "We're all cold and very hungry."

Caroline and Peter looked at each other, as if trying to read the other's thoughts.

"What do you think we should do?" Peter asked cautiously.

"Have you any idea where we are on the map?" Caroline asked.

He gave an embarrassed smile. "I thought I had about a dozen times, but I was wrong each time. Once you miss a checkpoint, you're doomed. All these valleys look alike."

"I know," Caroline admitted. "I thought we were heading due east to a checkpoint, because the sun sets in the west—"

"But it doesn't!" Peter exclaimed. "It's midsummer. It's more like northwest in the summer, you know."

"Oh," Caroline said. "That explains it." She glared at Peter. "Don't say it!" she threatened.

"I wasn't going to say anything. I'm just as guilty of stupidity. We decided to go around a hill instead of over it, because it looked a little too steep. We never did find the path again!" He grinned, his face suddenly transformed into a little boy's appealing smile.

"So what are we going to do?" Rachel asked.

"Do you think we should risk finding our way in the dark?" Peter asked Caroline.

Caroline shook her head. "We nearly stumbled over a cliff up there. We can't take risks like that in the dark. I thing we should stay put here. It's fairly sheltered, and they'll send out a party for us in the morning."

Peter grimaced. "We'll look pretty stupid," he began.

"I know, but I'd rather look stupid and bring all my campers home in one piece," Caroline confessed.

"You're right," he agreed. He turned to the kids. "OK gang, settle down here. We're going to spend the night here. Let's get some more wood for the fire. Think of it as an adventure. Pretend you're Indiana Jones."

"Indiana Jones would know the way back," one of the boys remarked.

"Anybody have anything to eat?" Peter asked.

Two candy bars were produced. Peter took out a pocket knife and divided them into six portions each. "Make the most of it. It's all you're getting until morning," he said. "And kids with jackets, you might share those with a buddy. Wrap them around two of you."

He lowered himself to a spur of rock and motioned for Caroline to sit beside him. She was looking at him with admiration at the easy way he had with his campers. She sank to the rock beside him.

"Here." He handed her a piece of Three Musketeers. "You want your dinner now or later?"

She smiled. "I'd like it now, but I guess I'll save it for an emergency."

"I'll save mine too," he said. "We'll make it a late-night snack!"

The night drew on. They attempted some campfire songs and some ghost stories, but Rachel became frightened. One by one the children dozed off or fell silent. Caroline sat, feeling the hard coldness of the rock digging into her back and her legs. She forced herself to keep her eyes open and stay alert. She had just dozed off when a twig snapped close by. Her eyes flew open. She stared out into the darkness. "What was that?" she whispered to Peter.

"What?"

"I'm sure I can hear something moving!"

"Probably just a squirrel or something."

"It sounded bigger than a squirrel."

They both listened. Over the night wind came a snuffling sound and rustling as something brushed through the undergrowth. Caroline swallowed back a scream and grabbed at Peter's arm. "What is it?"

"I don't know," Peter whispered back. They both listened as the sounds died away again.

"It's gone," Peter said.

Caroline shivered uncontrollably and found that she was still clutching to Peter. Embarrassed, she let go of his arm. "I'm sorry," she muttered, "but I'm tired and I'm frightened. I'm no good at this outdoor stuff. I guess I'm not counselor material."

Peter slipped an arm around her shoulder. "Come on," he said giving her a friendly squeeze. "You can't give up now. Not a girl who tosses rattlesnakes around."

"That really was a rattlesnake?" she asked, her voice trembling.

"It sure looked like one," he said. "You impressed me doing that. I would've run a mile away if the kids weren't watching!"

"I thought you were just teasing me," Caroline said. "I never dreamed ... *mon dieu*, I really threw a rattlesnake around?"

Peter laughed. It was a warm, comforting laugh. "Just shows you what you can do when you try," he said. "But then I suppose you go in for stuff like that at Berkeley. Are you one of those serious science majors?"

Caroline was very conscious of his arm, still tightly around her shoulder, sending warmth and comfort across her back. Suddenly it didn't matter any more whether she was a college student or not. Let them all know. After all, after today it probably wouldn't even matter.

"Look Peter," she whispered. "There's something you should know about me. I'm not a student at Berkeley. My cousin said that because everyone else was a college student and she didn't want us to be left out. I had to go along with it or make her look like a liar, but I've hated this whole thing."

"So you're not in college?" he asked.

"I'm going to be a high school senior next year."

There was a pause. She expected the arm to slide from her shoulder at any moment. Unexpectedly, there was the slightest chuckle.

"Me, too," Peter said.

"You what?" Caroline sat up, turning to stare at him.

"I'm like you—only in high school. Everyone else was sitting there talking about their colleges and their majors, so I decided no one would even want to know me if they thought I was just a little kid—so I said I was at UCLA. I live right there, so I know all about the campus."

In the flickering light of the fire, Caroline could see the amusement and relief dancing in his eyes. A very funny thought struck her suddenly: "Elizabeth would be really mad if she found out!"

"Elizabeth!" Peter's voice sounded scornful.

"I thought you and Elizabeth. . . ." Caroline said hesitantly.

"Elizabeth thought so, not me," he said firmly.

"But that evening at the campfire—I saw you with your arms around her. . . ."

"Correction, her arms were around me!" Peter said. "She asked me to get a bug out of her eye. While I was doing it, she wrapped her arms around my neck and started telling me how she wanted us to be real good friends. When I tried to answer, she kissed me. It seemed real impolite to just walk away while she was kissing me like that!"

Caroline started to giggle. "So you don't like Elizabeth?" she asked.

"I can't stand pushy women," he said. "It's a real turnoff to me if someone keeps following me around, chasing me. I don't like girls who come on too strong. They scare me." He paused. "Like your crazy cousin," he said at last. "Every time I look up, she's one pace behind me, pretending to need help! Is she always crazy like this?"

"She has her crazy moments, I agree," Caroline said. "She's not usually as crazy as this, though. She was trying extra hard to get you to notice her because"—she hesitated—"because we sort of had a . . . over which of us . . . but I backed down because it was too dumb and I thought you wanted Elizabeth anyway."

She was conscious of Peter's face, very close to hers, the pressure of his hand on her bare shoulder. "So you were fighting over me?" he whispered.

"Not really. It was only a joke," Caroline said. "At least, it was a joke to me."

"Thanks a lot!"

"I didn't mean it like that. I just thought that you were too stuck up to be my type."

"And what is your type?" he teased.

"Warm, kind, good sense of humor . . . the kind of person I can talk to easily . . ."

"Like we're doing right now, you mean?"

"Yes," she said with amazement. "Like right now."

His lips were only centimeters from hers. "You know what?" he murmured.

"What?"

"I think we've done enough talking for the moment," he said as his warm lips brushed against hers in the cool air. Gently at first, then firmly and warmly.

Chapter 14

The kiss seemed to last forever, until it was interrupted by a child whimpering in her sleep. Caroline and Peter drew apart hastily, looking at each other with that amused tenderness that comes from sharing a special secret.

Caroline sat up, checking on the sleeping bodies. "It's only Kendall," she said. "She's the one who gets the nightmares."

"Poor kid," Peter said. "I wouldn't have known what to do with her the other night."

"I didn't know either," Caroline said. "I couldn't wake her up, but afterward we just sat and talked together and she felt better."

"You seem to get along really well with the kids," Peter said. "I'm not used to little kids, except as a lifeguard at the beach. Then all I have to do is blow my whistle and tell them not to go beyond the buoys."

"I didn't think I was any good with the kids," Caroline said, "and tonight has really confirmed that."

"But you are," Peter said stroking her cheek so gently that she felt shivers all the way down her spine. "I watch you going around like a mother hen with all your little chicks scurrying after you, listening to everything you say."

Caroline gave an embarrassed giggle. "I felt like such a failure," she said. "I didn't realize how ill-prepared I was until I got here. I was the only one who didn't know the Outdoor Code!"

Peter laughed. It was a warm, secure laugh. "The guy next to me—that little nerd Howard whatsit—had written down the code. When Mr. Ed called on me, I peeked over his shoulder!"

"Really?"

"Cross my heart!"

Again their eyes met, casting a warm glow in the darkness.

"It's amazing how you can get the wrong impression about someone. Especially if you're insecure," Caroline said thoughtfully. "I was convinced you were this superconfident lifeguard type who could do anything and always had girls flocking around him. . . ."

Peter gave that appealing boyish grin. "You were right about the girls. I can't help it if I'm adorable—although you were the one person in camp who didn't seem to fall for my boyish charm."

"Because you always seemed to be putting me down, or putting Chrissy down."

"She deserved it," he said. "In fact, she was beginning to bug me. On that first day, when I met both of you, I tried to talk to you and she hogged the conversation. I thought you looked like the kind of person I'd like to know better. I thought, at first, that you were interested in me, too. But then your cousin was *everywhere* with you, and besides, you cut me down every time I tried to talk to you, so I figured I'd read the signals wrong and you didn't like me at all."

Caroline turned to look at him. "Oh, Peter," she said, shaking her head.

"Just think. If tonight hadn't happened, we might have wasted the whole summer, going around avoiding each other," Peter said tenderly, "and I might even have been forced into Elizabeth's arms."

"You said you couldn't stand her!" Caroline reminded.

Peter grinned. She could see his white teeth, shining in the first rays of the rising moon. "Even I can't resist temptation forever," he said. "It's very flattering when a gorgeous older woman flings herself at you!"

"So you do admit she's gorgeous?"

"Totally perfect," Peter said. He laughed, touching Caroline lightly on the tip of her nose, "But that doesn't mean that I like her. She also happens to be totally wrapped up in herself. I couldn't take much of that. I have to like a girl and be attracted to her." He took Caroline's chin in his fingers and drew her face toward him. "And you seem to fit on both counts," he whispered, giving her the lightest brush of a kiss as the fire flickered out.

Caroline gave a sigh of contentment and sank back against his shoulder. His body felt warm and comforting as she closed her eyes. *If this is a dream, I don't want to wake up*, she thought. *After I left Luke I began to wonder if I'd ever feel anything like this again. Now I do! I feel alive and tingling and safe at the same time. It's a great feeling. I can't believe it's really happening to me! Wait until Chrissy . . .* She broke off all thoughts of Chrissy. Chrissy would not be very pleased. Poor old Chrissy, stuck with poison oak, feeling miserable about that, and then finding out that her cousin had managed to catch the boy that she was chasing. *But I didn't catch him!* Caroline thought unhappily. *I wasn't chasing him at all. Everything just happened. It must have been written in the stars.*

Peter's hand was softly stroking her hair. She felt her worries slipping away. It didn't matter that they would be in big trouble tomorrow. It didn't matter that Chrissy would be upset. Nothing mattered, except this moment. She found herself drifting off to sleep.

"Wooo-eee, look at Caroline!"

It was only a whisper, but it was enough to bring Caroline back to consciousness. Her eyes opened, blinking in the bright light. The focused on Peter's bright blue tank top and his tanned neck. She raised her head. Her neck felt stiff from lying in one position. She must have slept on his shoulder all night! He was still asleep, his own head leaning against a curve in the rock, his long dark lashes resting against his cheeks. He looked so sweet and little-boyish that Caroline had to stop herself from bending down to give his cheek a kiss. Especially since she knew that figures were standing over her. She looked up at them.

Rachel and Kendall had crawled up to the rock where she and Peter were sleeping.

Kendall was eyeing her with suspicion. "I thought you said you didn't like him," she said.

"I didn't," Caroline said, fighting back the blush. "But now I do."

"I can see that," Kendall said.

"Hey, Caroline," Rachel said excitedly. "I slept all night up on a mountain and nothing happened to me. Wait till I tell my dad that I got lost in the wilderness and I didn't get eaten up by anything!"

"And you can tell him how brave you were too," Caroline said, smiling fondly at the little girl.

Peter stirred beside Caroline. "Turn the light off," he muttered. The girls laughed. He sat up, rubbing his eyes. "I feel like I'll never be able to move my neck again," he said. "Did I lie there all night against that rock?"

"I guess you did," Caroline said, "because I had my head on your shoulder all night."

He stared at her, his eyes holding hers in a big smile. "Good morning," he said. "I see we've got company."

"Yes, I think the kids are all awake."

Peter wobbled to his feet. "Then we should try to get back to camp, I guess," he said, offering his hand to help her up. "Do your legs feel like jelly, too?"

"More," Caroline said, rubbing at her thighs.

"The kids must all feel the same way," Peter said, "So how 'bout if I take a couple of my boys and we go out on a scouting mission."

"As long as you don't get yourselves lost," Caroline said.

"Don't worry, I'll leave a trail of crumbs," Peter said with a grin. "No, we won't go far, just up that hill. We'll get a good view from the top and we'll be able to wave at a helicopter if they send one."

Caroline watched him in the distance, noticing how easily he climbed from rock to rock, the way his fair hair blew out in the breeze . . . *I can't believe he chose me!* she thought in wonder. *Last night I felt like a failure, and suddenly today I feel like a million dollars!*

Peter and the boys had barely disappeared into the trees when her campers heard shouts coming from down below. Pretty soon the boys reappeared with Mr. Ed and two forest rangers in tow. An hour later they all were safely back at camp.

Everybody clustered around, giving them a big welcome.

"We were so worried about you," the other counselors remarked. "Nobody slept a wink last night, thinking that something terrible had happened."

"Your cousin was all set to go out and look for you by herself in the dark," Elizabeth said with a laugh. "We had to chain her down to stop her."

"We decided to stay put once it got dark," Peter said.

"Very sensible," Mr. Ed commented. "That's what the Outdoor Code tells you to do: Stay put and let people find you."

At mention of the Outdoor Code Peter turned and gave Caroline a wink. Caroline felt as if she would float right up into the sky with happiness. Peter liked her, no one seemed to be mad at her, and everything was just perfect. Now, if only Chrissy. . . .

"Where is Chrissy?" Caroline asked, "Is she still in the infirmary?"

"She spent the night there because she was tossing and turning so much she thought she'd disturb her campers," one of the counselors said. "The poor thing. She's one huge rash, all over!"

"I guess that's what happens to you when you go tramping through poison oak," Elizabeth said, tossing back her hair. "I'm glad you're back in one piece, Peter. I can't imagine how you could get lost. I suppose you had to stick around to help her group." She gave Caroline a scornful smirk.

"On the contrary," Peter said smoothly, "She saved me from a rattlesnake. Calmly picked it up from the middle of the group and threw it away." As he said it, he slid an arm around Caroline's shoulder.

Caroline could see Elizabeth wrestling with her emotions. Her lovely face retained its smile, but Caroline could see her dark eyes, glittering with fire. *If she were a snake, I'd be dead by now,* Caroline thought.

Elizabeth tossed back her hair. "Anyone crazy enough to go around picking up rattlesnakes does not deserve to be rescued," she said, as she stalked off. Caroline and Peter exchanged an amused grin.

"I'll go find Chrissy," Caroline said.

"And I'll go find breakfast," Peter said, giving her shoulder a squeeze. "You want me to save you some?"

"Yes, lots of everything!" she called after him. "I feel hungry enough to eat a horse!"

"That's good. That's what the hash is made of this morning!" he called back.

Caroline flew across the campgrounds, her feet hardly touching the earth. She pushed open the infirmary door. Chrissy was lying there, dabbing lotion on a scarlet arm. She zipped out of bed when she saw Caroline.

"Cara, you're safe! I was so worried!"

"Don't hug me!" Caroline warned, dodging out of Chrissy's way. Chrissy stopped laughing.

"Sorry, I got carried away. I'm sure you

wouldn't like poison oak, along with frostbite and exposure and exhaustion and insect bites . . ."

"It wasn't so awful, really. We're all hungry, but apart from that we survived very well."

"Did you hunt squirrels or something?"

"It was only one night, Chrissy! We divided a candy bar between us!" Caroline laughed easily.

"I'd have been so scared if that had been me," Chrissy said. "All alone with those little kids."

"I wasn't quite alone," Caroline said. "Peter's group got lost too, so we spent the night together." She was glad that it was so dark in the infirmary because she knew that she was blushing.

"You had to spend the night with Peter's group?" Chrissy asked. "Wasn't that a fate worse than death?"

"Not quite," Caroline said.

She opened her mouth to tell Chrissy all about it.

"Why couldn't that have been me?" Chrissy blurted first. "I'd have really appreciated the opportunity. It was wasted on you! You don't even like him!"

Caroline kept quiet as Chrissy sank back onto her bed and began dabbing at her rash again. "Boy, this poison oak is miserable," she said. "I didn't even feel this bad with the chicken pox."

I can't tell her now, Caroline thought. *She's feeling bad enough as it is. I'll let her find out gradually, when she's up and about again.*

"I'm going to eat a huge breakfast," she said.

"And then I'm going to take a long nap. See you later."

"Sure, Cara. See you later," Chrissy said, climbing back into bed. She looked so small and helpless lying there that Caroline was seized again by feelings of guilt.

Stop being so dumb, she told herself. *You like Peter. Peter likes you. It's as simple as that. Chrissy doesn't really come into this at all!*

Chapter 15

In spite of instructions to rest all morning, Caroline couldn't get any of her campers to stay in the cabin. They were all hyped up, enjoying their roles as instant celebrities. Caroline had to admit that she didn't feel tired either. She felt as if she'd just opened a very ordinary door and stepped into a surprise party, and from now on everything was going to be exciting. She paused in front of the bathroom mirror, attempting to comb the tangles out of her hair, looking at her sunburned nose, the mosquito bite on her forehead, and scratch on her face. *And he likes me!* she thought in amazement, remembering Elizabeth's perfection. *It was nice to know that life was full of unexpected miracles.*

She went back to the cabin where the girls

were playing bed-tag, leaping from bed to bed
while Rachel tried to catch them.

"OK, so you're not tired," Caroline said with a
smile. "Why don't we go down to the lake and
join the others. A good swim would cool us all
off." She didn't add that Peter would also be
lifeguarding at this moment.

The girls changed noisily, hurling insults at
each other the way sisters do. The night's adventure had turned them from strangers into one big
family.

Peter was sitting in his usual position on the
stool on the doc . Again Caroline was struck, just
as when she first saw him, by that special quality
he had. He was like some god or hero straight
out of Greek mythology. As her noisy group ran
squealing into the water, he turned and saw her.
His face lit up in a big smile and Caroline felt her
heart do a triple somersault.

She walked down into the cool water, feeling
the scratches and bruises of last night's adventure
tingling all over her body. She dived in, cutting
through the water in a smooth freestyle, appreci-
ating for the first time the swimming lessons her
parents had insisted that she take when she was
younger. She swam without pausing until she
could feel the cold, deep water in the middle of
the lake. She stopped, treading water and revolv-
ing slowly to gaze at the hills and the sky. Perfect,
how absolutely perfect everything looked. She
couldn't remember feeling so alive since
Luke. . . . The thought broke off, had she finally

begun to get over him? Would she soon reach a stage where she could think about him and not get a pain through her heart? If anyone could make her forget, Peter could.

She took in a deep breath and slid beneath the surface, down, down into the green depths. *I wonder how deep it is here?* she thought. *It's so clear, but I can't see the bottom. I wonder if anything lives down there.* It was not a comforting thought, and she eased herself toward the surface again, kicking hard as she made for the light. She gasped as something grabbed her, and something like strong tentacles wrapped around her waist. She took in water and broke the surface coughing wildly.

"Did I scare you?" Peter's face surfaced beside her. "I meant to do one of those underwater embraces you see in the movies!"

Caroline finished coughing and began to laugh. "I was just wondering if anything lived in that deep water when I was grabbed from behind,"she said. "You nearly scared the daylights out of me."

"Sorry about that," Peter said. "I guess I'll have to practice my underwater techniques a little more."

"Just don't take the girl by surprise next time," she said. "Two minutes ago you were sitting in the lifeguard chair. I hope you haven't neglected your duties in pursuit of me!"

"Elizabeth kindly took over," he said with a grin.

Caroline's eyes opened wide. "That was very nice of her!"

"Oh, believe me, she didn't know what I intended to do during my break," he said, with a mischievous glint in his eye.

"And what did you intend to do during your break? Caroline asked, her eyes teasing.

"Only this!" Peter said, slipping his arms around her and pulling her close to him as his lips fastened on hers.

"Peter!" Caroline fought him away. "Not here. All the kids are watching!"

"So? Give them a few pointers for later on!"

"We already have a bad enough reputation after last night," Caroline insisted, trying to break his strong hold on her waist, "And Elizabeth will be watching, too."

"So we'll give her a few pointers."

"She'll probably dive in and drown us both," Caroline said, glancing in the direction of the dock.

"I don't care what she does," Peter said. "I'm not letting go of you until you kiss me, and I'm a trained lifeguard. I can tread water for hours if necessary."

"You're terrible," Caroline said, laughing. "All right. I surrender. One kiss." She puckered her lips and touched his.

"That was it?"

"For now," she said.

"I'm not letting go for that," he said, squeezing her waist harder.

"OK. How about this then?" She kissed him long and tenderly this time, conscious of the feel of his body against hers and the double-time beat of her heart.

"That was much better," he said. "but you're right. I sense little eyes spying on us. Race you back to shore."

"No way," Caroline began, but he had already glided off, cutting through the water with powerful strokes. Caroline shook her head and followed. By the time she reached the shallows, he was already standing on the beach, arms folded, grinning down at her.

"What took you so long?" he teased.

She took his hand and climbed up the beach, panting.

"I'm in bad shape," she said. "You'd better give me some private swimming lessons."

"Well if you drown, I'm an expert at mouth-to-mouth resuscitation," he quipped, reaching for his towel and rubbing his hair so violently that spray flew up.

Caroline walked across the hot sand to her own towel. As she bent down, a shadow fell across her. She straightened up and saw Chrissy, swathed in a large white bath towel that contrasted violently with her red, puffy face standing in front of her.

"Chrissy!" Caroline looked up in surprise. "Should you be up and around? Are you feeling better?"

"The nurse said that some fresh air might be a

good idea," Chrissy said. "Besides, I've been away from civilization for too long." She spoke like a robot, not taking her eyes from Caroline's face.

"Is something wrong?" Caroline asked.

Chrissy continued to stare. "I saw you out there. You and Peter," she said. "So you managed to win after all."

"Chrissy, it wasn't a contest—"

"Oh, no. What about our bet? You pretended you didn't take it seriously and that you weren't even interested in him, when all the while you were waiting for the perfect moment. Well, you got it, didn't you? How did you work it to get lost with him? What a brilliant plan! I never thought you had it in you!

"Chrissy?" Caroline gazed at her cousin in horror, noting the steel gray eyes and the cold tone in her voice. Chrissy was not joking. She meant what she said. "Chrissy, you don't believe I got lost on purpose, do you?" she asked.

"Oh, no," Chrissy said with heavy sarcasm. "You just happened to lose your way and bump into Peter in the middle of the whole wilderness. What a coincidence! Of course it was planned, Caroline. I'm not stupid, you know. You think I'm a country bumpkin, but you can't fool me so easily. You're just slicker than me. I'm up front with people. You work underhandedly. That's the difference."

"Chrissy, listen to yourself!" Caroline said angrily. "You don't know what you're talking about! Do you really think I'm the sort of person who would plan all this just to trap a boy into liking me? It doesn't make sense."

"What doesn't make sense?" Peter asked, moving up behind Caroline and putting a hand on her shoulder. "How are you feeling, Chrissy? Did you hear about our adventure?"

Chrissy looked from Caroline to Peter and back again. "Yeah, I heard things got really close," she said. "I think I'll go find my campers. At least I can trust them!"

Chrissy turned and stomped back up the beach, ignoring Caroline's calls.

Caroline felt bad about Chrissy all afternoon, but she didn't think it would be wise to go after her. Chrissy needed time to calm down. Her famous hot temper usually took time to cool. Still, Caroline couldn't help feeling uneasy. Even though she was innocent of any of the scheming Chrissy suggested, she had ended up with the boy that Chrissy wanted, and that wasn't a very nice thing for a cousin to do.

So what am I supposed to do? she argued with herself as she dried off in the cabin. *Am I supposed to tell Peter that I can't be his girlfriend because it would upset my cousin? That's equally dumb. I'll have to make her understand that it just happened and she'll just have to learn to accept it.*

She finished dressing and followed the sound of the lunch gong. Her campers were already busy piling their plates high with bread and cold cuts. She joined them, feeling as if she hadn't eaten for days. Peter had saved her a seat at the counselor's table, and she slid into it gratefully. Brandon, Josh, and the other counselors at the table were full of quips and questions about the ordeal in the wilderness and disappointed to find out that everything was so ordinary.

"You mean no mountain lions attacked? No avalanches, no scorpion bites? Man, you could have jazzed this up before you came back."

"Sorry," Peter said. "It was bad enough as it was, worrying about not being found and hoping that the kids were going to be all right. Mountain lions and scorpions would have been too much—although we did hear a bear!"

"No kidding."

"I think they were too busy to notice anything," Brandon said, giving Josh a nudge.

"It does get kinda cold out there," Josh teased. Caroline envied Peter's tan. It was impossible to tell whether he was blushing or not, but she suspected he was as embarrassed as she was.

"Hey, cut it out, you guys. We had ten little kids with us all night."

"Oh, sure," Brandon said with a wide grin. "But little kids fall asleep."

"Trust old Pete to find the only way to get a girl alone at this camp!" Josh laughed. "I bet you had this getting lost business all planned out. We were struggling to follow those crummy maps and make it back before dark while you two were secretly meeting up on the mountain!"

"It wasn't like that at all," Caroline interrupted.

"We both got lost, and luckily we met each other before it got dark. Otherwise it would have been terrible, out there alone."

The boys still grinned, and Caroline really didn't mind their teasing anymore. It was teasing among friends, and she could tell that the other counselors were secretly impressed with both of them.

"I must try the same thing next year," Brandon said. "How about your cousin, Caroline? She's pretty cute. Too bad she has poison oak!"

"How about Elizabeth?" Josh added.

"Man, she'd eat you for breakfast!" Brandon quipped.

"Speaking of Elizabeth, where is she?" Peter asked, looking around.

"She said something about having to do some paperwork," Brandon said.

"Paperwork?" Peter asked, somewhat puzzled.

"Speak of the devil," Josh muttered, as Elizabeth headed straight for their table.

"Oh, there you all are," she said. "Peter and little Caroline. How sweet! It must have been a very interesting night up there on the mountain!"

Caroline winced under her sarcasm, but Peter remained cool. "It was," he said. "Too bad you couldn't have been there."

A couple of the other boys laughed. Elizabeth's smile clouded over for a second, then she turned it back on full force.

"I've been going through the files," she said.

"And I've just discovered something really interesting."

She waited for all the faces at the table to look up at her.

"Something you'd be interested to know, Peter," she continued. "You see, I pulled out Caroline's application form. Guess what? She doesn't go to Berkeley at all. She's only a little high school junior!" She let out a peel of laughter. "So you've been cradle snatching, Peter. Naughty boy."

Peter didn't take his eyes from her. "Did you go through all the files, Elizabeth?" he asked calmly.

"No, not all of them."

"Not mine?"

"Of course not."

"If you had," Peter said slowly, "you would have found out that I'm just a little high school kid too."

"You're what?"

"At that first meeting, everyone else seemed to be in college, so I said I was too. But I'm not. I go to Santa Monica High. I guess *you* were cradle snatching!"

The smile had finally faded from Elizabeth's face. "I don't believe it."

"Go check the records, which, incidentally, I'm sure you had no right to be doing in the first place."

Elizabeth's face was bright red. "You little creep," she said. "What a pair of little liars you are. You deserve each other."

"Why, thank you," Peter said. "I'm glad we have your official blessing!"

There was a murmur of laughter from the rest of the table. Elizabeth turned and stalked away.

Peter turned to Caroline, who didn't know whether to laugh or cry. "I guess that took care of her," he said.

He reached over and took her hand. "Hey, relax. It's OK."

"Peter, you didn't have to tell her. . . ."

"Why not? I'm not ashamed of good old Santa Monica High," he said. "Besides, everyone knows me now as I really am. If they like me as a person, they won't care where I go to school."

"You're all right, Peter," Brandon said. "You put that stuck-up creep in her place. She's been acting like she owns this camp."

"You see, Caroline," Peter said, squeezing her fingers. "Everything turned out fine."

"All the same," Caroline said softly. "She's an enemy I'd rather not have. I don't think she forgives and forgets very easily."

Chapter 16

"Dear Tracy,

I'm glad you're feeling better now and can go out again. It must be miserable to be stuck around the house when the weather has been so gorgeous. Up here the weather is a little too nice. It's been so hot most afternoons that all the kids have wanted to do is flop in the lake. They've all been getting really good at water sports, so there is stiff competition for the water carnival that's coming up. You'll be surprised to know that my cabin has the best four-person canoe team! I think we can even beat the boys.

It's hard to imagine that I've only been up here for three weeks. It seems like forever. Every day starts with a whistle blast at seven o'clock and the sound of a lot of little voices squealing.

(They've always got something to squeal about!)

Three whole weeks and I haven't lost a camper yet (although I came pretty close on a night hike when I got us all lost and we had to spend the night in the wilderness)! It was pretty scary at the time, but the results were not all bad: we became instant celebrities around camp; my kids decided that they didn't hate each other totally and they didn't hate camp totally; and, last but not least . . . I decided that I didn't hate a certain lifeguard called Peter Hamilton totally!

I know Chrissy must have written to you, so I'm sure you've heard all about Peter and how gorgeous he is! I agree with everything she's said. He's not only cute, he's very special—a truly nice person. (Also very cute—did I mention that?) I might even send a photo next letter. We sent some film off to be developed. I'm also sure she must have given her side of the story about how we got lost in the wilderness together. She was really chasing Peter in a big way, and she has not yet forgiven me for getting him instead of her. Honestly, Tracy, you know me—I am not the sort of girl who goes around chasing boys and trapping them! We got to know each other while we were stranded on this hike, and we sat and talked for hours. Chrissy thinks I got lost on purpose— can you believe it?

Actually she has been acting real strange since she got here. She did all kinds of weird things to make Peter notice her and the weirdest thing of all was that she totally turned him off. To top it all off she came down with poison oak! I felt very sorry for her because she was feeling so bad and she looked so terrible, but I don't know that I feel bad for her anymore because she is still going on and on about Peter and me!

Tell me honestly, do you think I should give him up because she likes him? Although she's recovered from the poison oak by now, she's still acting very cold toward me and sees me as a sort of rival in everything. When we have any sort of games or races, she has to beat me no matter what. You know how stubborn she is. She thinks I betrayed her! I don't know what to say to make things better between us. It's one of the only things that is spoiling what would otherwise be the greatest summer.

You asked in your letter whether I was still surviving in the great outdoors with my horrible kids. The answer is yes and yes. I know how to recognize all sorts of birds and animals (thanks to Sam, my nature buff). I've had a couple of run-ins with spiders and skunks, and almost a bear, but I knew I had to act calm and relaxed. How's that for bravery!

The rest of the kids have settled down now too. Kendall almost never threatens to phone her father. Rachel has blossomed after her night in the wilderness. She thinks that since she survived that, she can survive anything. Francesca is still a pain. I think she was born that way. I've never seen her laugh. And Jodi—poor old Jodi—uses me as Dear Abby and tells me all her boy problems—some expert!

Must go now—that's the bell for dinner. Our days up here are spent anticipating the next meal! We always seem to be hungry. Write soon. We love getting letters, and I expect you do too.

Your friend, Caroline"

Caroline folded the paper with a smile and tucked it into an envelope.

"Come on, Caroline! We're going to be last in the dinner line!" Kendall yelled as she ran past. Caroline got to her feet and followed, choking on the dust made by many pairs of feet all running to the dinner line together. Her campers clustered around her.

"We were down at the lake again. You should see Sam with the canoe paddle. She's a whiz!"

"She's totally awesome, Caroline!"

Sam looked uneasy but managed to smile.

"We're counting on you, Sam," Caroline said. "We're going to win the big canoe race."

Sam shrugged her shoulders, looking down at a trail of ants moving across the dust.

"Is something wrong, Sam?" Caroline asked. "Don't you want to be in the race anymore?"

Sam looked around uneasily again. "Elizabeth asked me to be in her boat," she muttered.

"Elizabeth?"

"Yeah. She said she can pick who she likes, because she doesn't have a cabin of her own. She said she'd pick the best team and we'd win."

"That creep!" Jodi muttered.

"You didn't say you'd go, did you?" Kendall threatened.

"Of course not," Sam said, "but she keeps on bugging me. And she keeps on saying bad things about Caroline."

"Like what?" Kendall demanded.

Sam glanced up at Caroline, then looked away, embarrassed. "She said that our team would never win the canoe race because you'd wimp out in the middle. She said you were a real wimpy type of person and that you became hysterical when you got lost on that hike and that Peter had to stay with you to save you."

"But you know that wasn't true, Sam," Caroline said angrily. "You were there."

"Yeah, I know," Sam said, "But she's always talking about you. I don't know why."

Caroline managed a convincing smile. "I do," she said. "Pure jealousy. Don't worry about it. It doesn't upset me, so it shouldn't upset any of you." *I really won't let it upset me!* Caroline decided.

"I hate her," Rachel said fiercely.

"I said don't worry about it," Caroline said. "We'll show her when we beat her fair and square in the canoe race, right?"

"Right!" the girls said, dancing happily around again.

The line moved forward toward the food table. Caroline could see Elizabeth's black dancing curls at the front of the line.

I forgot to tell Tracy about Elizabeth, she thought, *and how she can't resist getting in constant little jabs about me all the time. She's really beginning to get on my nerves, but I won't give her the satisfaction of knowing that she's bothering me. If only Chrissy and I were on better terms, I could tell her about it. It's bad enough having Elizabeth as an enemy. I don't need Chrissy against me, too!*

Elizabeth laughed loudly, and Caroline couldn't help wondering if the joke was on her. *You are getting too sensitive,* she told herself firmly. *What does it matter what Elizabeth says about you? People are not dummies. They know you're OK, you know you're OK, and Peter likes you, so what else matters?*

Elizabeth swept past the line, carrying a tray piled high with food. She stopped next to Caroline's group and smiled. "Last again, huh, Caroline? Did you get lost on your way up from the lake?"

Her ringing laugh echoed across the compound as she walked away with her friends.

"Don't worry, Cara. We'll show her," Sam muttered. "I won't be in her crummy boat, whatever she says."

They arrived at the food table, and Caroline saw Brandon making frantic gestures in her direction. "Over here, Caroline. We've saved you a seat!"

She carried her tray across and dropped down

beside him. She noticed that Chrissy was sitting across the table.

"Hi, Chrissy," she said brightly. "How was your morning? How is your team coming along?"

"Fine, thanks," Chrissy answered politely. "And my team is great—good enough to beat your team, anyway."

"I don't know about that," Caroline answered, still brightly. "We've got a couple of whiz kids on my team. Little Sam is stronger than all the boys, and she's canoed a lot before, which really helps."

Chrissy still looked at her with no sign of emotion on her face.

"Do you have anything you need mailed, Chrissy?" Caroline asked. "I'm going to hitch a ride down to the store after lunch and mail a letter. I'll pick up the mail, too. I haven't had a letter for three days. Do you want me to pick up yours while I'm there?"

She could tell that Chrissy was torn between wanting her mail, and not wanting Caroline to do a favor for her. "OK," she growled, managing a half smile.

We're getting somewhere at last, Caroline thought. *That is the first time she's smiled at me since the fight.*

"And where's the famous Peter?" Brandon asked cheerfully. "Don't tell me you two have been separated all morning?"

Caroline giggled. "He's been trapped in that lifeguard chair for hours. Everyone wants to practice for the water carnival nonstop. I guess he's going to grab a sandwich down there."

Chrissy got up. "I'm done," she said. "See you guys." And she walked off without looking back.

"What's eating her?" Brandon asked. "Is she still feeling itchy?"

"I guess so," Caroline answered, not bothering to mention that it wasn't just the poison oak that made Chrissy such a grouch.

After lunch Caroline rode down on the truck into the tiny town at the end of the dirt road. She mailed Tracy's letter, bought supplies of jelly worms, which had become currency around camp, and picked up the mail. There were two letters for Chrissy and one for her from her parents. Chrissy took the letters without uttering a word.

"Oh, come on, Chrissy," Caroline said, her patience finally stretched to a snapping point. "Why don't you cut this out! You can't stay mad at me forever, you know. We've been such good friends."

"Until you blew our friendship by putting a knife in my back." Chrissy said in a clenched voice.

Caroline turned away, not knowing what to say to make things better. "I'll see you down at the lake, I expect," she said.

"Sure," Chrissy answered. "You think you're going to beat me there too, don't you? You're so sure of yourself these days. Well, if you win, it's only because you got yourself the best canoe!"

"Chrissy, you are being totally childish," Caroline said angrily. "If you want my canoe you can have it. All the boats are the same."

"No, they're not. The yellow one is faster!" Chrissy said.

"So have the yellow one. I really don't care," Caroline said, walking out of the cabin and leaving her cousin alone.

"Why are we using the blue boat?" Caroline's team demanded as they stood on the beach, ready to begin the water carnival. The swimming races and other water events had been going on for nearly two hours. Now the sun was glowing red in the sky, and the canoe races were starting.

"It doesn't matter what color boat we use," Caroline said. "We're the best team."

"So why can't we use the yellow boat?" Kendall wanted to know. "We practiced in that one."

"Because somebody thought that boat had an advantage, and I wanted to show that we can win no matter which boat we use."

"Right!" Sam said forcefully. "Let's go get 'em, gang."

"Ready!" they all growled. Caroline had to hide her smile. Were these the same bored, timid little girls who had arrived at camp only a short time ago?

The teams dragged their canoes to the water's edge and climbed in. Mr. Ed, standing on the dock, called out starting instructions. Out to the yellow buoys, around them, and back again. Peter, standing beside Mr. Ed on the dock, gave

Caroline an encouraging wink. The gun sounded. Paddles moved in unison, the canoes skimming over the water as spectators screamed and cheered. Caroline sat in the stern of her canoe, steering a straight course to the buoy. Only a few yards past the dock and already they were ahead! She could just see the yellow nose of Chrissy's canoe out of the corner of her eye. *So much for the fastest boat!* she thought with a smirk.

They paddled on, every paddle rising and falling at the same time, every muscle straining until the boat moved so fast it felt as if it were flying. The girls paddled so smoothly that Caroline had a sensation that the water was streaking past them while the canoe sat perfectly still. The yellow buoy was up ahead. They had practiced the manuever so many times that they swung effortlessly around it. The other boats were nowhere near it yet. Chrissy's was next, but not close enough to give them a good fight. Elizabeth had obviously decided not to enter this race after all. Maybe nobody wanted to be on her team!

Caroline's team could sense victory. Sam, at the bow, picked up the pace. Suddenly there were screams behind them. Caroline looked back in time to see Chrissy's canoe in the process of rounding the buoy, rock unsteadily, then capsize as if a hand had reached up from the water to pull it over.

For a moment all Caroline could see was a yellow hull and the unbroken water surface around it.

"Chrissy!" Caroline screamed. "Turn around!" she yelled to her crew. "We're going back!"

"But we're winning!" Kendall complained.

"And they're drowning!" Caroline yelled. She was jamming her paddle hard into the water. She swung the canoe around in a tight circle stroke so fast that she thought her arm muscles would snap. One or two heads had already broken the surface and were thrashing wildly near the over-turned canoe. Chrissy's was not one of them.

"Help them aboard," Caroline commanded, "and hold the boat steady." A second later she climbed over the edge of her canoe into the water. *Chrissy!* she thought. *Just hang on until I can get there!* She remembered that Chrissy was not the best of swimmers. She had almost drowned under that wave on the beach near San Francisco. Caroline could see the shadow of the hull above her and pairs of wildly thrashing legs. One pair of legs she noticed thankfully, was longer than the others. She came up beside Chrissy and found her with her head under the canoe. She was safely above the water line, clinging onto the upside-down seat.

"What are you doing in here? You had me scared silly when you didn't come up!" Caroline complained. Her voice boomed and echoed uncannily in the confined space.

Chrissy turned a white face to her. Her eyes were wide with terror. "I don't know how to swim under water, Cara. I'm scared of getting my face wet."

"You just have to duck your head under the side, Chrissy. Only two strokes and you'll be safe. Just hold your breath and I'll lead you, OK? You can even shut your eyes if you like."

Chrissy continued to cling. "I can't," she whispered.

"Well, you can't stay here forever," Caroline said with a smile. "Come on, Chrissy. I promise I won't let go of you. You'll be fine."

Just then there was a splash nearby. In moments, Peter's head appeared under the boat with them.

"Mind if I join the party?" he asked with a grin.

"Did you bring the chips?" Caroline asked, overwhelmed with relief to have him so close to her.

"No, but there's plenty of drink," he said. His lighthearted smile faltered. "Do you realize you just gave me heart failure?" he asked Caroline. "I saw you dive in, and I kept waiting for you to come up!"

He looked at Chrissy. "Are we all hanging out here for a purpose?"

Caroline opened her mouth to speak, then shut up. She didn't want to put Chrissy down again in front of Peter—especially not then. "Chrissy got the wind knocked out of her when she hit the side of the boat," Caroline said. "She was just taking a rest to get her breath back."

"Kind of cozy under here," Peter said. "One of the perks of being a lifeguard—all alone with two beautiful women."

"Shouldn't you be saving the others?" Caroline asked.

"All safe and accounted for in your boat," he said. "You were the only two missing in action."

"Ready to come out now, Chrissy?" Caroline asked, suspecting that Chrissy would rather die than admit to Peter that she was scared.

"OK," Chrissy said in a small voice.

"We'd better help her, in case she still can't breathe properly," Caroline said, taking Chrissy's arm. "Ready, one, two, three, go!" Before Chrissy could protest, she was swept down and up again, propelled to the surface by strong arms. Mr. Ed was standing by in the motor launch and hauled them all aboard.

"I can't imagine what went wrong," he said. "Nobody was standing up, and these little canoes are usually so reliable."

On the shore the kids clustered around while Caroline helped her cousin onto the beach.

"Are you OK now?" she asked, holding her own towel out for Chrissy.

"That's your towel. If I use it, you might get poison oak," Chrissy said in a small voice.

Caroline smiled. "I'll risk it," she said. "I don't want you to suffer from shock."

Chrissy sank onto the warm sand. "You're right. I do feel cold," she said. "I was pretty scared back there."

"Anyone would be," Caroline said, sitting down beside her.

"No, not anyone. Only a klutz like me," Chrissy

said. "I've screwed up every single thing I've done since I came to this camp. Most of all I've screwed up my friendship with you. You saved my life just now. And you gave up your own chance of winning."

"Chrissy!" Caroline cut in. "Do you honestly think I would put a canoe race before your safety? A crummy little canoe race?"

"But the way I've been behaving . . ."

"We're cousins," Caroline said. "We have family ties here. It's the code of the hills to rescue each other!"

"What hills?" Chrissy asked, beginning to laugh. "San Francisco hills? I thought the code there was to run people down with your BMW!"

"That's better," Caroline said. "It's good to see you laughing again. I thought you were going to stay mad at me forever, and that really hurt."

Chrissy gave a little smile. "I guess I'm a sore loser," she said.

Caroline gave her shoulder an affectionate pat. "No boy is worth our friendship," she said. "If you're all right, I'd better go and talk to my girls. I hope they're not too mad about losing the race."

She walked over and squatted down beside them. "I'm sorry, gang," she said. "I made us forfeit the race, but you know we really were the best. Maybe we'll get another chance. . . ."

They looked at her and nodded. "It's OK," they all mumbled. "We couldn't let people drown."

"It's strange, isn't it," Sam said, "that the yellow boat flipped over today. It's always been fine before. It was almost as if it were weighted all wrong." Her eyes met Caroline's—innocent, little-girl eyes that said quite clearly, "Everyone thought we were getting the yellow boat."

Caroline nodded. "I'll get Peter to check into it, secretly," she said. "It does make you think that perhaps—"

"Perhaps Elizabeth was mad and she wanted to make you look like a fool again. Tipping over on the turn would do that very nicely," Sam commented.

"You think Elizabeth did it?" the other girls whispered, horrified.

"Don't say anything," Caroline whispered back. "We can't prove anything."

They got up, muttering among themselves. Caroline watched them, hoping that they wouldn't stir up trouble before she was completely sure. They didn't go near Elizabeth. They went off together down the beach. The carnival went on. Boys fought each other with foam baseball bats on a pole until one got knocked off, falling into the water with a loud splash. Soon it was time for the counselor's canoe race. Caroline opted to sit it out with Chrissy. Elizabeth took her place in the small, one-person canoe, beside a line of male counselors. She looked back at Caroline and laughed. "Couldn't face the competition?" she called.

The gun sounded, and the line of canoes moved forward. Elizabeth was stroking wonderfully. Her canoe sped across the water, ahead of all the others—until it reached the edge of the dock. Then it appeared to stay where it was, even though Elizabeth was paddling just as hard as ever. Gradually a ripple of laughter moved through the spectators. Caroline walked down to the water's edge and quickly saw the reason for it. Elizabeth's canoe was fastened to a long rope, which was attached to a concrete block on the beach. She had reached the end of the rope and didn't seem to realize that she was going nowhere. The giggles became shrieks and soon howls of laughter. The whole group watched as Elizabeth looked around and saw the rope stretched taut behind her. They watched her face turn beet red and her mouth utter angry words.

Caroline glanced across at her campers. They were standing slightly apart from the others and exchanging looks of pure delight. Caroline walked over to them.

"Well?" she asked.

"That will teach her to be so mean to you," Kendall said.

"If anyone asks, you don't know how the rope got attached," Sam instructed her.

"I guess it got there the same way the uneven ballast got in the canoe," Caroline said innocently. They all dissolved into noisy laughter as they walked back to the cheering, jeering crowd.

Chapter 17

Caroline stood alone in the bathroom, combing through her wet hair, reflecting on the events of the afternoon. Over a space of one half hour, she had experienced both terror and elation, and the conflicting emotions had left her drained.

What I wouldn't give for a hot shower, she was thinking.

"Caroline? Are you in there?" The familiar sound of Chrissy's voice echoed around the tiled walls.

"Mmm-hmm," Caroline called around the rubber band she held in her mouth.

Two seconds later Chrissy's head appeared. "Oh, there you are. I've been looking everywhere."

"I take it you're recovered!" Caroline said with

a big grin, wrapping the band around her damp ponytail.

"Recovered? I've never felt better!" Chrissy said. "In fact, I feel as if I could float up and touch the stars!"

"I'm glad to hear it, Chrissy," Caroline said. "I really can't stand it when you're angry with me. It makes me miserable."

"I'll never be mad at you again, I promise!" Chrissy said, "Because the reason I was mad is all over and forgotten."

She waved a letter into Caroline's face. "Guess what this is!"

"A letter?" Caroline asked cautiously.

"From Jeff!" Chrissy yelled. "He wrote to me. Your mother forwarded it. He says it's very lonely on the tour and he misses me and he thinks about me all the time!"

"That's great, Chrissy!"

"And that's not all." Chrissy's whole face was as bright as the North Star. "He's going to be playing in Reno. He didn't know I was up here, and he wondered if I could drive up from San Francisco to see him. But I'm only about an hour away, Cara. I can't believe I may be seeing him again so soon."

"So we're not rivals any more," Caroline said.

"You can have Peter with my blessing," Chrissy said. "And Cara, I'm sorry I acted like such a jerk. I've been thinking about it all afternoon. I was a total, complete, utter jerk, wasn't I?"

"Well, you did overreact a bit," Caroline acknowledged.

"At least I understand why now," Chrissy said. "It was the backlash from losing Jeff. When you got the boy I was making such a big play for, I began to worry if what you said was true—if I did only get boys by accident. I began to worry that I'd never have a boyfriend again and that I'd be an old maid."

Caroline laughed. "Some chance of that!"

"But you know what I mean," Chrissy said. "My self-confidence was shattered. Everything I did made me look stupid. Then I crowned it all by getting poison oak! That made me feel so terrible that I wasn't myself. I said some terrible things to you, Cara. Can you forgive me?"

"Already forgiven," Caroline said.

"So now you and Peter can have a wonderful time here without worrying about me," Chrissy said. "And without worrying about Elizabeth, after today. I don't think she'll bug you again. In fact, when her uncle examines that boat, she may be sent packing."

"Poor Elizabeth," Caroline said, her voice dripping with sarcasm. "I guess she was as insecure as the rest of us, only she managed to hide it better."

"Another good thing," Chrissy said, "is that you're finally over Luke. You've found a guy to take his place. Now I won't have to put up with dreamy looks and long sighs—unless they're about Peter, of course."

"Hold on a minute," Caroline said. "Stop going so fast. I really like Peter, but let's leave it at that for now. For one thing, I have a feeling he has a girlfriend back home. He hasn't exactly mentioned her, but I've gotten hints. And for another thing, I can't shut Luke completely out of my mind. I don't know if I ever will be able to, but I'm sure as heck going to have a good summer up here with Peter. He's fun and he's nice and he's certainly cute, and if it only lasts as long as this camp—well, that's what was meant to be. I'm not going to worry about it."

Chrissy looked at her with admiration. "Wow, you sure have grown up recently."

Caroline laughed uneasily. "Maybe it's having the responsibility for all those little kids. In a way, I'm glad we had no idea what we were getting into before we got here. If we had, I'm not sure I would have shown up."

Out in the twilight a guitar was playing, and voices joined in a rowdy campfire song that echoed from the cliffs.

"We'd better get out there," Chrissy said. "Maybe you and Peter can ride up to Reno with me, and we can go on a wild, crazy date together!"

"Maybe," Caroline said.

"And maybe Jeff will come back here to visit and we'll take a boat out on the lake—only not the yellow one—and it will be so romantic with the moon and everything. . . ."

Caroline laughed. "It's nice to have you back,

Chrissy," she said. "Let's go. Your little dears will be wondering what's happened to you."

"And Peter will be wondering what's happened to you," Chrissy said.

"Right," Caroline said, with a big sigh of contentment. "I'll see you later." She hesitated for a moment, then wrapped her cousin in a tight bear hug before she turned and ran to join Peter by the campfire.

Here's a sneak preview of *Surf's Up!*, book number eight in the continuing SUGAR & SPICE series from Ivy Books.

"I just got some great news," Tracy said, looking from Chrissy to Caroline. "My parents were worried that I wasn't getting better fast enough, so they called my aunt last night and asked her if I could go and stay with her until I get my strength back. My aunt said YES!"

"That's great, Tracy." Chrissy beamed. "You must be really close to your aunt."

"Are you kidding?" Tracy asked, wrinkling her nose. "My aunt is super-strict. I have to be in by ten o'clock when I stay with her. But . . ."

"But what?" Caroline pressed.

"She lives in Hawaii. Who would turn down a couple of weeks in Hawaii?"

"Wow!" Chrissy exclaimed. "You lucky thing. All those cute guys on the beach would make anyone take an interest in life again."

"If my aunt even lets me go to the beach," Tracy said, rolling her eyes. "She probably won't let me out of her sight without a chaperone."

"Do you have cousins out there to hang around with?" Caroline asked.

Tracy shook her head. "My uncle and aunt don't have any kids. They're a nice, quiet, elderly couple, unfortunately."

"Bummer drag," Chrissy said, trying out the phrase she had picked up from some of her campers. "I guess Caroline and I had better come along to keep you company then, right, Cara?"

"Hey, wait a minute," Tracy exclaimed. "Why *don't* you guys come along? That would be fantastic!"

Caroline made a face. "And all our college money would go right down the drain."

"But it wouldn't cost that much," Tracy insisted, leaping up from the bed excitedly. "Just your plane fare and spending money. You could eat and sleep at my aunt's house."

"Right," Caroline said with a grin. "Your aunt will really want to put up with two strange girls, as well as her niece."

"I'm sure she wouldn't mind," Tracy said. "After all, if you two were there, she wouldn't have to worry about letting me out alone. I know she'd let me go to the beach with my nice, reliable friends to look after me."

Caroline snorted with laughter, but Chrissy had wriggled off the window seat. "I don't know what you're laughing about," she said to her cousin. "I think it's a *terrific* idea. We'd be great chaperones for Tracy, we'd be able to help her meet all the cutest boys and . . . holy cow!"

"What?" the other girls demanded, as Chrissy broke off with a wild yell.

"Do you know who's in Hawaii right now? I can't believe it—my dreams are all coming true! Jeff is actually there with his band; I'll be able to stroll down moonlit beaches, hand in hand with Jeff, just as I imagined it."

Tracy shook her head, smiling. "You haven't met my aunt yet. You and Jeff and my aunt will be strolling down the beaches together."

"I don't even care," Chrissy said, beginning to pace the room like a caged panther. "Just being with Jeff again would be the most wonderful thing in the world. You know, I was so depressed because I thought we wouldn't be able to spend much time together before I leave, and now, suddenly, out of the blue, wham! All my wishes are answered. I must have a fairy godmother someplace. Let's call your aunt right now, Tracy, and ask her if Cara and I can come along, too. Come on, I'll help you dial."

"Chrissy!" Caroline touched her cousin lightly on the arm. "Hold on a minute, okay? Come down to earth."

"What's the matter?" Two worried faces turned to stare at Caroline.

"We need to do some thinking about this whole thing, that's all," Caroline said, sitting back on the bed and fiddling nervously with her hands. "We can't just go rushing off to Hawaii, you know. Think this over logically. You do need money for college, and I thought you were going to hang around here until Jeff gets back."

"But that's nowhere near as good as being with him in Hawaii!" Chrissy replied, her eyes shining.

"Come on, Caroline," Tracy joined in. "What's the matter? Don't you want to come with me?"

"Of course I do, Tracy," Caroline said, "but I'm trying to think of the future, too. I need money for college as much as Chrissy does. The airfare to Hawaii alone would take a big bite out of my earnings. I'd love to go on vacation right now, but . . ."

"Fine," Chrissy said. "*I'll* go with Tracy and you can stay home and save money. We'll be just fine without you. It'll be great in the surf, getting swept away by giant waves and eaten by giant sharks. They'll probably send you back the part of my bikini that they found washed up on the beach. You'll look at it and say, 'If only I'd gone along to take care of Chrissy. If only . . .'"

"All right! I'll go!" Caroline exclaimed. "You've talked me into it."

"Hey, this is exciting," Tracy said. "We'll go surfing and snorkeling . . ."

"And go to beach parties and get the world's greatest suntan," Chrissy continued, going over to sit beside Caroline on the bed. "Come on,

Cara. Aren't you just the teeny-weeniest bit excited?"

A big smile began to spread across Caroline's face. "Just a teeny bit," she agreed, jumping up. "Come on, Chrissy, let's go home right now and decide what clothes we have that would be right to take to Hawaii!"

ABOUT THE AUTHOR

Janet Quin-Harkin is the author of more than thirty books for young adults, including the best-selling *Ten-Boy Summer* and *On Our Own*, its sequel series. Ms. Quin-Harkin lives just outside of San Francisco with her husband, three teenage daughters, and one son.